STA

A sudden noise ... ... Anna's heart to a stop. Someone was fitting a key to the lock and opening the front door. . . . Footsteps approached quietly and a figure appeared beside the desk. . . . How could he not see her? Then he turned toward the desk, and did.

For a second he stared at her without understanding, face blank with shock. Anna leaped to her feet. He said, "Goo' gawdawmighty!" and stepped back to the doorway, tripped, and fell flat on his back. His cigarette landed on the back of his donkey jacket.

He was supine, blocking the way to the back. The front door was locked. She thought momentarily of throwing herself, like a stunt man, through the window. But at the sight of all that bric-à-brac massed in front of it, the thought died. There was nothing left but her wits and they were suffering from shock.

She bent down and picked the cigarette off the intruder's chest.

"Your coat's burning," she murmured. "Better put it out."

Agatha Christie

Death on the Nile
A Holiday for Murder
The Mousetrap and Other Plays
The Mysterious Affair at Styles
Poirot Investigates
Postern of Fate
The Secret Adversary
The Seven Dials Mystery
Sleeping Murder

Dorothy Simpson

Last Seen Alive
The Night She Died
Puppet for a Corpse
Six Feet Under
Close Her Eyes
Element of Doubt
Dead on Arrival

Elizabeth George

A Great Deliverance
Payment in Blood

Colin Dexter

Last Bus to Woodstock
The Riddle of the Third Mile
The Silent World of Nicholas Quinn
Service of All the Dead
The Dead of Jericho
The Secret of Annexe 3
Last Seen Wearing

Michael Dibdin

Ratking

John Greenwood

The Mind of Mr. Mosley
The Missing Mr. Mosley
Mosley by Moonlight
Murder, Mr. Mosley
Mists Over Mosley
What, Me, Mr. Mosley?

Ruth Rendell

A Dark-Adapted Eye
  (writing as Barbara Vine)
A Fatal Inversion
  (writing as Barbara Vine)

Marian Babson

Death in Fashion
Reel Murder
Murder, Murder, Little Star
Murder on a Mystery Tour
Murder Sails at Midnight

Dorothy Cannell

The Widows Club
Down the Garden Path
coming soon: Mum's the Word

Antonia Fraser

Your Royal Hostage
Oxford Blood
A Splash of Red
coming soon:
Cool Repentance
Jemima Shore's First Case
Quiet as a Nun

Stalker
by Liza Cody

BANTAM BOOKS
NEW YORK · TORONTO · LONDON · SYDNEY · AUCKLAND

STALKER

*A Bantam Book / published by arrangement with
Macmillan Publishing Company*

PRINTING HISTORY
Macmillan edition published 1984
Bantam edition / December 1989

ISBN 0-553-18503-9

Published simultaneously in the United States and Canada

PRINTED IN THE UNITED STATES OF AMERICA

O   0 9 8 7 6 5 4 3 2 1

Chapter 1

'What had happened,' Anna explained, walking down the avenue of newly green trees, 'was that his wife had sneakily married a twenty-three-year-old economics student. But for the ten months in question she was still raking in the maintenance.'

'Clever,' Selwyn murmured. 'I wonder if I could con Bea like that—while eating lotus with an eighteen-year-old dancer, I mean.' He weaved towards her and away again. Even sober, Selwyn had trouble walking straight.

'You couldn't con Bea,' Anna said realistically, 'and I doubt if you could pull an eighteen-year-old dancer either.'

'Father figure?' Selwyn suggested hopefully.

'Not a chance.'

'Cuddly?'

'Cuddly's not enough these days.' They walked on to where Holland Park ended abruptly opposite the Kensington Odeon.

'Anyway,' Anna continued, turning left up the High Street,

1

'at first this chap was so outraged that his wife had taken up with a younger man he could scarcely speak to me. I thought he was going to tear the report up into bite-sized morsels and feed it to me.'

'But you charmed him into a sweeter mood.'

'Better still, I pointed out how much money he'd be saving. So he cheered up and took me out to dinner.'

'Perhaps he fancied taking up with someone younger, too.'

'Yuk!' Anna said disgustedly. 'You know what he ordered? Quail. And the waiter brought four of them all laid out like premature brown babies on a dish. He only ate the lot! And what do you think the schmuck does for a living? He photographs birds for glossy mags and calendars. He's supposed to be an ornithologist. Do you think I could be interested in a geezer who needs four dead birds for one course of one meal?'

'No, but you could be interested in a geezer who can afford them.' Selwyn grinned slyly.

They arrived at a place where Anna had only to cross the road to be at the office. Stuck for a suitable insult, she made a rude gesture with two fingers of her right hand and waved it at him in farewell. She turned away and waited for a gap in the traffic.

'Anna!' Selwyn was still dithering behind her. 'Anna, what the hell am I doing out here on a Wednesday morning?'

'You were going to the library,' she told him patiently. 'Harlech. Remember?'

'Oh, that's right.' His faced cleared, only to wrinkle again almost at once. 'Um, you don't happen to remember what I was going to look for, do you?'

She couldn't help him there, so he wandered off irresolutely hoping it would come to him when he got there, his shirt-tail hanging below the hem of his jacket. He was doing some research for Harlech Television, and a poet unwillingly on his way to make an honest crust was a sorry sight.

She crossed the road and the pavement, and went into a dark doorway hidden between gaudy Indian prints on one side and over-priced gents' footwear on the other, and ran up the stairs two at a time. At the top Beryl, already making spaghetti of the switchboard, tapped the face of her wrist-watch and pursed her vermilion-coated lips. Twenty-five to nine. Late. Caught.

'And by the by, Anna,' Beryl said, as though she had already spoken. 'The Commander wants a word. I found this billy-doo on the typewriter when I came in.' She passed over a square of paper which read, 'A.L. see M.B. 10 a.m. Advise.'

There was only one M.B. in the firm of Brierly Security and unfortunately only one A.L. Anna hoped it wasn't about her Auto Use claims and went down the corridor to the Rec room for a cup of coffee. Bloody Beryl: tough as old boots, but with all the sensibilities of a maiden aunt in her armoury too. On top of that, she flirted with the boys: an unnerving combination.

It was full house in the Rec room when she got there: Johnny, Tim, and Phil reading morning papers, studying form and raising smoke signals with their cigarettes, Bernie blowing on his coffee, rocking gently on the back two legs of his chair.

'Morning all,' Anna said, dumping her coat on the bentwood coat-stand by the door. Except for Bernie's 'Hello, love' a series of grunts in varying keys answered her. Already there was powdered milk and powdered coffee in her mug. She had only to add water from the steaming kettle. She sat down between Johnny and Bernie and peered over Johnny's shoulder. The page he was reading was devoted to what had happened at Newbury the previous day. Sometimes she bought a paper of her own and joined the general morning silence, but it was not a regular part of her routine. Bernie, on the other hand, got up early and read his at breakfast. But that was Bernie, always managing to fit everything into its proper place.

She stopped peering, and Bernie said, 'What're you up to today, love?'

'I don't know yet,' she said, taking a mouthful of the brew in her mug. It had only heat to recommend it. One day, she promised herself, she would break herself of the office coffee habit. After all, she always had genuine coffee at home before leaving for work. And Beryl only bought the cheapest ersatz for the hired hands. It was better when someone remembered to bring in fresh milk. But nobody had bothered that morning.

'I'm seeing the old man at ten,' she went on, 'but he hasn't said why.'

'New client maybe,' Bernie said, still rocking.

'Hope it's not an Arab this time,' Phil said, looking up. Everyone except Anna sniggered. They were recalling a memorable occasion when a dignitary from Qatar had objected loudly to a woman being made privy to his confidential business. A good deal of reshuffling of jobs had resulted from that one, which left Anna at the bottom of the roster again. It had caused a lot of amusement among the men, whose opinion of a woman's ability was not much different from the Muslim one.

'It won't be,' Johnny said confidently. 'The old bastard never makes the same mistake twice.'

'We don't want to embarrass the clients with dreadful things like legs and faces,' Tim said, imitating the old bastard so well that even Anna laughed. Phil, Tim and Johnny automatically glanced at Anna's legs before returning to the racing results. It was all normal.

By nine, everyone else had drifted away, and Anna went out to buy milk. She made another mug of coffee and spent the next hour polishing her report on the ornithologist's ex-wife and padding her expenses as much as she dared. At ten, she went along the corridor to Martin Brierly's office.

This was the showpiece of Brierly Security, giving the impression of stern efficiency and confidentiality that Martin Brierly thought his clients liked to receive. It overlooked Kensington High Street, but was cut off from any rising clamour by double-glazing. Brierly's desk was large and bare. There were hard upright chairs for the clients, and the walls were decorated with detailed maps of London and the home counties.

Martin Brierly sat behind his desk with his back to the window. He was a large man with a round head. His thinning brown hair was brushed flat across his scalp so as not to spoil the shape of a perfect sphere. He said, 'Ah, good morning, Miss Lee. You already know Mr Chivers.'

Max Chivers was a solicitor who often used Brierly Security when his clients needed a small, conservative firm of private detectives. He was white-haired, in his sixties, and thought of himself as a country gentleman. He favoured hairy tweeds and smelly pipes. He and Martin Brierly usually understood each other perfectly.

'Nice to see you again, Miss Lee,' he said, standing up and extending a soft, pink hand. 'Let me introduce Mr Thurman.'

Mr Thurman murmured 'How do you do,' turning his face towards her so that light strobed off his spectacles in a meaningless heliogram. His spectacles were so thick that when she could see his eyes, they were magnified out of all proportion to the rest of his face and looked like huge blue fish in a small goldfish bowl. When he turned back to Martin Brierly, his eyes seemed to recede as well and swim away to the back of the bowl. He sat meekly in his hard chair, hands folded monk-like in his lap.

Not the aggressive type, Anna thought, relieved. Some clients, feeling themselves to be in alien territory, reacted with a show of dominance and tried to tell everyone how to do their jobs. Others put themselves entirely in the hands of the experts and passively gave up all responsibility. The second group, though easier to deal with, were no more realistic than the first. It took two to tango, Anna thought. An agent's performance was dependent on good instructions and detailed information. A solid contribution by the client could make a world of difference when it came to sorting out his problems.

'Well now, Miss Lee. I'll bring you up to date,' Brierly said, placing both hands flat on either side of the new cream client file. He would already have made himself familiar with Mr Thurman's case, explained Anna's qualifications, and, most important of all, discussed terms long before she arrived. 'Mr Thurman has unfortunately fallen among thieves. About eighteen months ago an acquaintance of his, one Edward Marshall, approached Mr Thurman for a loan. Marshall claimed to be a skilled carpenter and wanted to set up a workshop where he could make bookshelves, kitchen fittings, that sort of thing.'

'Reproduction country furniture in pine,' Max Chivers elaborated. 'There's quite a demand nowadays.'

'Quite so,' Brierly said with a trace of impatience. 'It appeared to be a sound investment. Mr Thurman would be a

6

partner as well as financier. He advanced a sum of money for Marshall to hire premises and buy equipment.'

'Jigsaws, routers, that sort of thing,' Max Chivers put in. 'It was quite a considerable sum.'

'Marshall, of course, supplied Mr Thurman with details of how the money was spent, and all appeared to be satisfactory,' Brierly went on. 'A further advance was necessary to provide materials for demonstration models and advertising.'

'After a suitable period, my client of course wished to see the workshop,' Max Chivers said, 'to satisfy himself that the money had been well spent and that Marshall was properly set up for business. An appointment was made and . . .'

'As you can guess,' Brierly interrupted, refusing to be robbed of a punchline, 'the premises were occupied by strangers who had never heard of Marshall. Marshall, of course, vanished. All this took place in Birmingham.'

'Birmingham?' Anna said, alarmed. She had only been to Birmingham twice, and on both occasions had got lost. She was not over-keen to work there.

'My home town,' Mr Thurman said apologetically, and settled back to let Max Chivers talk for him. Max Chivers obliged. He said, 'With some difficulty, my client has traced Marshall to London: Kilburn, to be exact. He has a furniture shop there; bought, no doubt, with my client's money.'

'The problem is that Marshall appears to have gone away again,' Brierly said.

'Temporarily, we hope,' Max Chivers put in. 'Mr Thurman has other business in London and cannot spare the time to wait until he returns.'

7

'Well, fine,' Anna said, looking from Brierly to Chivers and back. The double-barrelled explanation appeared to be over. 'That seems straightforward enough.'

'Very straightforward,' Brierly said. 'Mr Thurman has been kind enough to supply a photograph of Marshall, so you should have no trouble recognizing him.'

'Does Marshall have a family in Birmingham?' Anna asked. 'Might he have gone back there for a while?'

'Apparently not,' Brierly said. 'Mr Thurman has been unable to find any sign of him there.'

'Did you employ inquiry agents in Birmingham?' Anna asked Mr Thurman, curious to know if he would answer a direct question himself. He did not. Max Chivers said, 'Yes, he did. They discovered nothing more than that he had moved lock, stock and barrel to London.'

'Is he married? Does he have a home address in London?'

'I'm afraid not,' Max Chivers said. 'The shop in Kilburn is as far as my client has been able to pursue the matter.'

Anna was surprised that anyone as helpless as Mr Thurman had been able to pursue it that far. She said, 'What do you want me to do when I find Marshall?'

'I think that's where I come in,' Max Chivers said, taking out his pipe and all his smoker's paraphernalia and putting them on Brierly's desk. He started to pack his pipe. Long strands of tobacco escaped and fell on to his knee and from there to the carpet.

'Ashtray, Miss Lee,' Brierly said wearily. He was accustomed to Max Chivers's messy relationship with his pipe. It had little to do with smoking and a lot to do with spreading tobacco, ash and burnt matches randomly over the surroundings.

'Thank you,' Max Chivers said courteously, when Anna

had supplied him with the biggest ashtray she could find. 'Yes. We need to find Edward Marshall so that I can start proceedings. Restitution must be made. And failing that, prosecution.'

'I need hardly add that circumspection is the key-word. Marshall has disappeared once, and would probably do so again if he knew he was being looked for.' Brierly watched Max's pipe-lighting activities with some anxiety. He was worried that the singed box of Swan's Max used as a damper would catch fire. Anna thought he worried needlessly. Max Chivers rarely managed to get the tobacco to burn successfully, let alone the box of matches.

'You might have to employ er—er, a cover story,' Mr Thurman suggested tentatively. 'I hope you don't mind.' There was a trace of an accent, Anna thought, but not from Birmingham. It sounded more like Australian or South African and was so faint that she could not be sure. She said, 'If it's necessary.'

'It is, I'm afraid,' he said, enlarged eyes blinking weakly. 'I'm sorry I can't be of more help. I'm—er—rather occupied at the moment.'

'Leave it with us, Mr Thurman,' Brierly said, tearing his gaze away from Max Chivers's pipe. 'I'm sure Miss Lee will manage something.'

'Where can I get in touch with you?' Anna asked.

'Through me, of course,' Max said, sucking lustily.

'I'm afraid I have another appointment,' Mr Thurman said hesitantly, looking at his watch.

'My dear chap, you should have said so earlier,' Max Chivers said amiably, beginning to collect his equipment and distribute it in various pockets. The men exchanged pleasantries and Beryl was summoned to show the clients out. Anna wondered why Mr Thurman had bothered to come at all. His contribution had been almost nothing. Perhaps Martin Brierly had insisted on meeting him.

Chapter 2

Umbrellas were up in Kilburn High Road. There was no muscle in the rain, just the general air of damp and chill made solid. It sent the women scurrying into Safeway's for relief and unneeded packets of biscuits. Babies in water-proof-covered pushchairs steamed gently as they slept and were rattled along at an unseemly pace as their mothers hurried about their business.

Anna pulled up her collar, settled her gaberdine hat more firmly over her eyes, and turned quickly into Priory Park Road. Another turn to the right and she was there.

It was a shabby little shop flanked on one side by Patel Pharmacy and on the other by Drew's Auto Spares. A hand-written sign on the glass door said, 'Closed for Lunch.' It looked as if it had been there a long time. Anna squinted through the dusty glass. Second-hand furniture lay around like tombstones. There were some ancient porcelain chamber-pots and old stoneware hot-water bottles, but the impression was of a shop that couldn't make up its mind. One or two pieces looked like country pine but as far as Anna could tell they were old and had been stripped.

Drew's Auto Spares was closed for lunch too. Anna went into the chemist's. A white-coated assistant was stocktaking near the door, so she said, 'Excuse. me. Can you tell me when the second-hand place next door opens?'

'So sorry,' the man said, scarcely looking up from his clipboard. 'Can't tell. Sometimes nobody there all day.' And then as Anna turned to go, he went on more brightly, 'You want cheap furnishings? My brother has very good shop two streets down. Patel Fittings. Very good. Most inexpensive. Always someone there.'

Anna thanked him and left. She sheltered in the doorway of the launderette directly opposite. It wasn't a bad area, she thought; no residents' permits required, and not too many yellow lines. If she was going to have to hang around indefinitely, it might be a good idea to bring the car. While she was still deciding, a man approached and said loudly, 'Be not cast down. God loves you as He loves all sinners.'

'*Je ne comprends pas*,' Anna said, turning away quickly.

'Oh hell,' the man said, 'Well, *Dieu vous aime*, then.'

'*Merci*,' she said, making off at a fast trot. That settled it. She would go home, have lunch, and come back with the car. It was always happening. Women who loitered in doorways were sitting ducks for passing freaks. In the course of her work, Anna often found herself loitering in doorways and therefore attracted more than her fair share. It was a most unwelcome hazard to someone who needed to be inconspicuous.

A few years ago, when she had been on the Force, the uniform had offered protection from some types. But it had acted as an irritant to others. Anna had hated the uniform. She had hated the way people had reacted to it and not to the woman wearing it. It was something she hadn't thought about properly when choosing the police as a career; a choice she had made for all the wrong reasons.

That she had looked to the police for excitement and adventure said a lot about the restrictions and petty respectability of home life in her early years. To begin with, admittedly, she had enjoyed working outside and meeting people. She had also liked being at least partly responsible for her own decisions. The police was not like the army in that respect. And there had seemed to be a lot of variety in police work. But after a while, when she noticed that she attracted a lot of jobs where good typing was the only qualification needed, and where filing things in alphabetical order was a key to success, her enthusiasm faded.

But the most galling thing of all had been the uniform. She abhorred the fact that everyone knew at a single glance what she did for a living, but worse than that, everyone felt they could make assumptions about who she was, what she was like, and what she thought about. There was something in her nature that rebelled against being so easily and sometimes wrongly identified. The uniform had made her personally vulnerable to whatever any Tom, Dick or Harry felt about the police in general. She might have persevered had there been more compensations. But the exciting jobs that could have made it all worthwhile seemed to pass her by. Perhaps she just worked in the wrong district. Other women in other districts had no complaints.

Looking back, she did not think of her time on the job as time wasted. She had, after all, learned to be self-reliant there and unafraid of the outside world. And, given her family background, she recognized these as valuable lessons. Her regrets were more that she had not been allowed to give as much as she felt she had to offer: that in some respects, she had left the police still untried.

The Prices' ground-floor flat was empty when she got home. Selwyn was presumably still at the library, and Bea would not get back from work till half past five. She went upstairs and let herself into her own apartment. It was pleasant to be able to come home in the middle of the day, put a record on the hi-fi and wander around making tea and sandwiches. It would not go down on her worksheet, of course, but then she would not spend more than an hour on it either. Just being at home made it seem like a stolen hour.

When she had finished eating, she locked up and left, taking with her a carrier bag full of dirty clothes. The launderette had looked warm and clean and opportunities for doing the weekly wash while on the job were too rare to be ignored.

Back in Kilburn, the 'Closed for Lunch' sign was still in place. Anna went next door to Drew's Auto Spares which was now open for business. First she inquired about a float chamber gasket she needed for the Renault 4. There wasn't one in stock, but the owner said he could get it easily. While he was writing down the details, Anna said, 'By the way, do you know when Mr Marshall will be back? I wrote him a note and slipped it through next door's letter-box, but he hasn't replied. There never seems to be anyone in.'

'I haven't seen him next door for ages,' the man said, tucking his pencil behind his ear. 'I don't know where you'd find him. His wife goes in sometimes, and there's the lad who helps with the heavy stuff. But that place is more closed than open these days. I'm surprised he can make it pay.'

'Does he live above the shop?' Anna asked. 'Only I wanted him to see a chest of drawers I was thinking of selling.'

'There's an Irish family lives up there. Sorry, can't help you.'

Across the road, Anna put her washing into a machine and settled down to wait. But Edward Marshall's shop remained deserted. He didn't seem to have got much with Mr Thurman's money, Anna thought. Perhaps, as Martin Brierly had hinted, Mr Thurman hadn't parted with as much as he had claimed.

'He seemed a little gullible for a moneylender,' Anna had said when Mr Thurman had gone.

'I don't think he's exactly a moneylender,' Brierly replied. 'According to Chivers, he only occasionally puts money into a small business when he thinks it has a chance of success. Not such a stupid thing, the economy being as it is. All the same, people who invest money without proper precautions must expect to come unstuck sometime.' Spoken by one who would never let a penny leave his hand if it weren't chained to the wall, Anna thought.

She sighed and took the clothes out of the washer and put them into the drier. It was quiet in the launderette now and the manageress seemed disposed to chat. Her gray hair was arranged in aggressively tight curls all over her head and her busy feet brought her closer to Anna as she wiped and tidied, glancing at her from under the spangled rims of her glasses. Finally she said, 'I haven't seen you here before. It's a bit like a little village, round here. I get to know most of the people who use my machines quite well.'

'I expect you would,' Anna said with an encouraging smile. Maybe this was where Edward Marshall brought his dirty socks. On the whole, she doubted it. He glared out of his photograph, chin raised, with the sort of arrogance that stated quite clearly that he thought he was a man's man. Dirty socks would be Mrs Marshall's concern. It was one of Anna's quirky rules of thumb that a man with long sideburns was unlikely to help with household work, whereas a man with a beard might. Edward Marshall's sideburns extended an inch or so below his earlobes, but his chin was clean-shaven. Perhaps she should try the hypothesis out on the manageress. Someone who worked in a launderette every day would probably know.

Instead she said, ''Well, maybe you'd know when the shop over the road opens. I've got a couple of bits and pieces I want to get rid of, and I thought they might be interested.'

'I wouldn't bother with them,' the manageress said. 'There's never anyone there hardly. I don't think they bother any more.'

'Why on earth not?' Anna asked. 'It looks like a good location to me.'

'You should've seen it when old Mr Silver had it,' the manageress said regretfully. 'Like Aladdin's cave it was then. Mind you, he was one of the old school: loved trading, he did. They don't know what work is now.' And to prove her point she flicked her wet cloth across the top of the nearest machine, sending a little shower of soap powder flying into the air. Anna sneezed and said, 'I can't think why anyone'd bother buying a shop and then not trading.'

'He isn't the type, if you ask me. You need a lot of patience running a shop. He always struck me as the impatient type. Bored to death after a few months.'

'You know him then?' Anna asked without much hope. Opinions and hard facts seldom went hand in hand in this sort of conversation.

'Not to speak to,' the manageress said, cheerfully confirming Anna's suspicion. 'You can tell a lot by watching, though.

Not that I'm nosey. She might've made a go of it. Big strong woman like that. But not him, no.'

The drier abruptly stopped its churning, and Anna opened it. Her laundry smelled slightly of gas and hot rubber. She began to fold the things and put them back in the carrier bag.

'There's a coloured gentleman a couple of streets down who buys and sells second-hand,' the manageress said, looking critically at Anna's underwear. 'They say he's very good.'

Chapter 3

'That great, grey sponge in the sky's still being squeezed,' Selwyn complained, biting a huge semi-circle out of his wedge of fruit cake and staring moodily at the streaming window-panes. 'We should move to Greece.' Crumbs settled like dandruff on his Fair Isle cardigan.

'Why Greece?' Bea asked. She had her shoes off and her feet up on the sofa, hoping for a few quiet moments between earning a living and starting the housework. Anna had been called down from upstairs to mend the electric kettle which had failed suddenly at a crucial point in tea-making.

'What I need is bright light and air dry enough to sting the mucous membranes,' Selwyn said. 'This spring has no bloody bounce in it. What do you say, Leo?'

'You're going to need a new element,' Anna said, fiddling with the smallest screwdriver. 'I've patched it up for now, but it won't last.'

'Thanks, Anna,' Bea said without opening her eyes. 'I

don't know what we'd do without you. Have some more cake.'

'We could take a little white house on a steep hillside and grow olives and goats and drink Retsina all night. How would you like that?' Selwyn said, warming to his idea.

Bea opened her eyes and stared at him. She said, 'I'd grow the olives, Anna'd get the goats and you'd drink all the Retsina. We might as well stop at home for all the change that'd make.'

Selwyn snorted and banged out a line of Xs on his Olivetti. 'Well, it'd be a change for me, woman,' he said, sending the carriage back with a decisive hand. 'My brain's getting as soggy as the bloody weather.' He embarked on a line of Ws.

'I wouldn't blame the weather for that,' Bea said dangerously. 'If it's drying out you want, you could try walking past the off-license once in a blue moon.'

'You've no bloody imagination,' he complained. 'How about the movies, Leo? There's a late-night Horror on at Notting Hill Gate.'

'Not me,' Anna said, getting up. 'I've got to get out early tomorrow. I want to trap a postman.'

'You're no fun,' Selwyn moaned, starting to type, 'No fun, no fun, a postman, an island, a highland, a film and a fang but no fun,'

'Oh hell,' he said, staring with concern at the paper. 'I've gone and dropped a sultana down the whatsit. It's lodged between the hooha and the dodab. Help!' Anna went over and helped, smothering a fit of giggles. She loved the way Selwyn suddenly ran out of words at the end of a working day.

The postman came at eight. Anna was parked, waiting, close to Marshall's shop when she saw him turn into the end of the street. She got out of the car and went to meet him. The postman was a pessimist. He was wearing a raincoat although so far the morning was dry.

'Morning,' Anna said, falling into step with him. He had the rhythmical gait of a man who doesn't like to be stopped in the middle of something. 'Can you tell me where the man who owns the furniture shop lives?'

'Which one would that be?' the postman asked, shifting a bunch of letters from his hand into a greengrocer's letter-box without breaking his stride. He stepped off the pavement and aimed himself at a private front door across the road. Anna followed, saying, 'Mr Marshall: second-hand shop next to the chemist.'

'What you want to know for?' He slid letters through two doors in a row and then set off in a diagonal towards the launderette.

'Dresser in the window. I'm interested, but the shop's never open, so I thought I'd try him at home.'

The launderette upset the postman's rhythm as the letterbox was right at the bottom of the door. He had to stop and bend down to get the letter through. When he stood up, he looked irritated and Anna added insult to injury by putting herself directly in his path.

'Mr Marshall?' she repeated, smiling but standing firm.

'Tadema Road,' he snapped, scowling. 'Don't ask me what number. I can't remember.'

She stepped aside and he continued on his way. After a few paces he got into his stride again and his face cleared.

Anna went back to the car and set out to find Tadema Road. It wasn't far; a narrow street of terraced houses each with a front garden the size of a small blanket. It amazed her that anyone could have the enthusiasm to be inventive with gardens so tiny, but some of them were decked out like miniature Hampton Courts. Others, of course, were completely neglected, the whole space being taken up by an overgrown box or laurel hedge.

Marshall's house was behind one of these. His name was on the bottom doorbell, indicating that he had the groundfloor flat. She had wheedled the number out of a paperboy who had in turn wheedled a small backhander out of her.

Curtains were drawn tightly across the front window. As it was still only eight-thirty, Anna sat in the car and waited.

At ten o'clock the curtains were still drawn. Anna went to the door and rang the bell but there was no reply. She rang the two bells above Marshall's but they drew no response either.

The postman's pessimism was justified: it began to rain quite heavily. Anna drove to Marshall's shop and found it exactly as she had left it—'Closed for Lunch.' She was wet and bored, and the morning wasn't even half over. There was nothing more entertaining to do than phone the office.

She told Mr Brierly Marshall's home address and then said, 'No one's seen him in the shop for months. They say his wife goes there sometimes but the house looks deserted too.'

'It's rather premature to come to that conclusion,' Mr Brierly said, sounding bored too. 'Keep an eye on both places for a couple of days. Talk to the neighbours. But keep a low profile.'

Anna really did not see how she could successfully do both so she rang off and went to find a café where she could have a cup of tea and think about it. Being unobtrusive was her stock in trade. Drive the average car. Wear clothes that fit the circumstances. Too much make-up gets you noticed. None at all could get you noticed too. When you talk to someone, be slightly boring; then they'll give you information and be pleased when you go. Sometimes shock tactics work, but only occasionally. If you want to get away with being professionally nosey, unremarkable is the effect you should try to achieve.

At one time she had thought this might be a romantic job. But people with romantic illusions find it hard to make a living.

Anna went back to Tadema Road just in time to see, at the window of what she supposed to be Marshall's flat, a woman with a head of champagne-coloured curls. She was standing side-on to the window, talking to someone Anna couldn't see. Anna went and sat in the car, watching the front door.

Action at last. Her mood lifted.

After a while two men, both with raincoat collars turned up and hat brims pulled down against the rain, emerged from the front door. They walked down Tadema Road towards Kensal. Anna took their place on the doorstep and rang the bell. This was not exactly talking to the neighbours. Nor was it being unobtrusive. But it was something to do after a day and a half of dreary waiting.

The woman with champagne curls opened the door. She was tall and shaped like a figure eight. In earlier years, she would have worn a corset. As it was, she filled her blouse and slacks like wind in a spinnaker.

'Mrs Marshall?' Anna beamed enthusiastically. 'Mrs Edward Marshall?'

'Who wants her?' the woman said, her full mouth tightening with suspicion. She was in her late twenties or early thirties, blue-eyed and plump-cheeked. A slightly undershot jaw gave her a stubborn look, but except for the cold stare, she was very attractive.

'This is the right address, isn't it?' Anna let the beam slip a fraction. 'We hate to make mistakes with our lucky winners.'

'I'm Mrs Edward Marshall,' the woman said. 'Jane Marshall if you want to know. What you talking about, lucky winners, anyway?'

'It's Mr Edward Marshall I want to talk to, actually. He wouldn't happen to be at home, would he?' Anna peeked coyly round Jane Marshall as if her husband might be hiding behind her.

'He's out,' Jane said. 'What's he won anyway? He don't go in for competitions as a rule.'

'The Aston Martin proved a great temptation,' Anna said brightly. 'We had literally thousands of entrants. When will he be in?'

'He's away on business,' Jane said uncertainly. 'You telling me he's won a bleeding Aston Martin?'

'Of course we'd need to verify his *bona fides* first. Talk to him. But I'm sure it'll be all right. It nearly always is. When do you expect him home?'

'Well, I can't say, exactly.' Jane Marshall looked upset. 'Won't I do? I'm his wife, after all.'

'It's a question of comparing signatures, little things like that,' Anna said helpfully. 'We do have to be careful with our big winners. Mistakes cause such ill feeling, and ill feeling is bad publicity. If you could let us know where he is, we could get in touch and then you wouldn't have to wait.'

Jane Marshall looked distinctly unhappy. she said, 'Are you sure I won't do instead? Because he was going round the auctions in the West Country, so I don't know where you'd find him.'

'Who wants to find him?'

Anna turned round sharply. One of the men she had seen leaving had come back.

'Edward's gone and won a bleeding Aston Martin,' Jane Marshall said defensively.

'Who are you, anyway?' He had reddish hair showing in untidy strands under his hat. Narrow cheeks and yellowish teeth gave him a foxy appearance. He did not look friendly.

Anna said, 'Well, I represent the distillery. Of course they don't run the competition themselves. It takes competition specialists. Not everybody knows that.'

It was a lost cause now. She cursed silently and turned to Jane Marshall. 'I'm sorry Mr Marshall isn't at home,' she said, keeping the wide smile in place. 'Perhaps you'd like to get in touch when he returns. I'll leave you my card.' She found a card in her bag. It had her name on it and her home telephone number. Nothing else. Yellow Teeth snatched it out of Jane Marshall's hand and examined it. Jane looked anxious.

'Goodbye, then,' Anna said cheerfully, slipping past Yellow Teeth on to the pavement. 'I look forward to hearing from you shortly.' Instinct made her walk past the car and carry on up Tadaema Road to Kilburn.

Chapter 4

Anna ate supper alone in front of the television. Selwyn was composing what he referred to as a latterday dithyramb. He did not explain too succinctly what a dithyramb was, but Anna gathered that it had something to do with the Greeks, Bacchus and the fruit of the vine. Selwyn's poetry often had a lot to do with the fruit of the vine. He had clearly been getting himself in the mood all afternoon and, when Anna said it just looked like an ordinary drunkard's raving to her, he chased her back to her own flat with outraged cries of 'Illiterati' and 'O-Level Dummkopf'. Bea, not unnaturally, had a headache.

Anna cleared up the supper things and switched the TV off. She had a bit of poking around to do before bedtime.

Martin Brierly had not been pleased with her tactics. 'That was rather impetuous, Miss Lee,' he had said, revolving his thumbs at top speed.Impetuousness was considered close to stupidity.

'At least we're further on than we were,' Anna said quickly.

'His wife obviously doesn't know where Marshall is. I mean she isn't hiding him or anything. She wanted that Aston Martin.'

'Beware of premature conclusions,' Mr Brierly said, regarding her with a look that said plainly he thought her a dangerous nonconformist. 'What did you make of the man?'

'I don't know,'' Anna confessed. 'A brother? Someone looking out for her while her husband's away?'

'If Mr Marshall has defrauded Mr Thurman,' Mr Brierly said patiently, 'it's not unreasonable to suppose he might have served others similarly. We might not be the only people looking for him. You say the wife seemed uneasy with this man?'

'A bit.'

'Well then.' He allowed himself a satisfied smile.

So Anna had gone back to Marshall's shop and waited inconspicuously but in vain. Towards the end of the afternoon, when the shop keepers were locking up, she wandered around and found an alleyway dividing the yards behind the shops from the yards of the buildings in the next street: a sort of service access. But not much used, Anna thought. The alley was too narrow for lorries or large vans, and the yard fences looked neglected. She peered at the yards through holes and loose slats until she found one that looked like Marshall's. There was a pile of old timber, some badly broken chairs, the rusting springs of a couple of beds, and a pile of something covered by tarpaulin. The gate was locked, but the fence looked just steady enough to climb. It was still daylight, so she went home.

Now she put on a pair of black cords, trainers and a navy blue anorak. She was about to be impetuous again. She wondered briefly why. She was usually careful and methodical. Spring fever, she thought, as she left the flat and padded quietly downstairs. Selwyn was right, it was the sort of spring that made you restless, impatient for summer. The month was right, the trees were greening up nicely, but it rained persistently. It was like a protracted cold that would not let go. It made her want to shake free and run south to the sun.

During the familiar route to Kilburn, she watched the windscreen-wipers swish right and left and thought there would be no rubber left on them if the weather didn't improve soon.

She left the car at the end of the alley. In her pocket were a rubber-covered torch with most of the glass masked with Elastoplast, three sizes of screwdriver and a sturdy square of stiff plastic. If these didn't do the trick, she would give up and go home without a stain on her conscience. The breaking half of breaking and entering was not part of the plan.

She knew what she was about to do was illegal, unethical and risky. Worse, Martin Brierly would have a fit if he found out. But he was not going to find out. It was just that she knew a stagnant situation when she saw one. If she had read the signs right, and she was certain she had, she could be hanging around the launderette for weeks, until Mr Brierly or Mr Thurman decided to call her off.

She counted yard gates and then looked through a gap in the fence to make sure she had come to the right one. Then, after looking quickly around to make sure no one was watching, she jumped and hauled herself up to the top of the fence, swung her legs over and let herself down on the other side. She hung by one arm while she used the torch swiftly to see if she was about to land on a pile of tin cans. There was nothing but an empty patch of concrete, so she let go and dropped silently to the ground.

No dogs barked. No neighbours leant out of windows shouting, 'Oi, who's down there?' It was just a normally quiet London night: traffic sound, TV sounds, voices safely tucked away behind glass and curtains. And probably, all over London, there were hundreds of people, just like her, advancing stealthily on back doors that weren't their own.

The back door to Marshall's shop was half glass. It had shrunk in its frame, and the old Yale lock was loose. Anna was almost annoyed with him for making it so easy. She couldn't understand why people did not protect themselves better. It always took a thief to show them how easy they were to steal from.

She left the door open and took a few cautious paces into the passage beyond. For a minute or so she stood motionless, listening, then crept to the front of the shop. A door to the left stood ajar. She shone the torch quickly into the room. It was empty except for a few lumpy mattresses and a stack of chairs. Another half glass door led into the shop itself.

It was dimly lit by the street lamp outside the window. This was a problem. Anyone looking into the shop would be able to see her moving around. Anna crouched, and in this position opened the door. Keeping low, and with a wary eye on the window, she moved forward and to the right until she was shielded from sight behind a massive office desk. It was the desk that interested her. She knelt so that her head would not be visible and started to go through all the drawers.

She found some screwdrivers, pliers, nails, tacks, bits of broken moulding, crumpled tubes of wood glue, cloth, polish, Brasso. But judging by the lower drawers, whatever else he did, he did not make furniture. Not here at any rate.

The top drawers were stuffed with paper: old bills, invoice books, advertising sheets, envelopes, a magazine called *Sol-*

diers of Fortune, all higgledy-piggledy. The petty cash box contained elastic bands and drawing-pins. There was a desk diary, but it was for the previous year. Anna searched, but could find nothing for this year. In fact, except for the cash books, there was nothing else worth looking at.

She sat cross-legged and opened the diary. The first thing she noticed was that there were no entries after the beginning of October last year. The existing entries were mainly times with initials scrawled beside them or just the initials. Sometimes there were jottings like, COD 25-50 or Wd 6-37 or 6Cs 10-50 the lot. Prices, she supposed. The last entry was for October 5th, and said simply 'B & S'.

Tucked between the pages all through the book were auctioneers' flyers. The last one was headed Bailing and Sparrow, Frome. The date of the auction was October 5th. B & S, presumably. On September 29th was another entry and another corresponding auction sheet. This one was headed Galvin, Cox and Ross, also in Frome, and several items on it were starred. Anna folded both sheets and put them in her pocket. Then she went through the diary more carefully.

Marshall had been to several sales that year. Anna concentrated on the ones in the West Country. He had gone there once in February and then again in June. On both occasions, there were no other entries made in the book until two or three weeks after the last sale date. Once down there, it seemed, he liked to stay.

She put the diary back where she had found it and opened the account book. This was a mess. In the first column were descriptions of articles, barely readable. The second column contained the price they had been bought for, and the third, what they had been sold for and a date. The fourth column was reserved for profit. It should have been a simple system but, as well as being nearly illiterate, Marshall also had trouble with his arithmetic, and the figures were scratched out, rubbed out and generally blotted beyond recognition.

Anna was just flipping to the back of the book to see when the last entry had been made when a sudden noise nearly brought her heart to a stop. Someone was fitting a key to the lock and opening the front door.

A draught of fresh air flooded the shop and, horrified, Anna heard the back door click shut. She switched off the torch and sat like a stone, scarcely breathing.

The shop bell was stifled before it had a chance to ring and then the door was closed and locked. Footsteps approached quietly and a figure appeared beside the desk, moving towards the rear of the building. If Anna had reached out, she could have touched his trouser leg. He opened the door into the passage. There were soft scuffling noises. Then a match rasped. A whiff of cigarette smoke came back into the shop. Without turning her head Anna could see out of the corner of her eye a dim yellow glow.

Footsteps again. The trouser legs stopped close by. How could he not see her? Then he turned towards the desk, and did.

For a second he stared at her without understanding, face blank with shock. Anna leaped to her feet. He said, 'Goo' gawdawmighty!' and stepped back to the doorway, tripped, and fell flat on his back. The candle flew out of his hand and hissed and died on the damp floor. His cigarette landed on the front of his donkey-jacket.

He was supine in the passage, blocking the way to the back. The front door was locked. She thought momentarily of throwing herself, like a stunt man, through the window. But at the sight of all the bric-à-brac massed in front of it, the thought died. There was nothing left but her wits and they were suffering from shock.

She bent down and picked the cigarette off his chest.

'Your coat's burning,' she murmured. 'Better put it out.'

He said, 'What? Oh,' in a strangled gasp and flapped his hand ineffectively at his front.

'Here, let me.' Anna banged masterfully on his chest. 'That's better.' The patch on his donkey-jacket stopped smouldering. The shop was scented with the smell of singed wool. She retrieved the candle and gave it to him. He sat up and whispered, 'What are you doing here? There ain't no money. You nearly frightened the life out of me.'

'Same here,' Anna said with deep feeling. He lumbered to his feet. 'Come in the other room,' he said. 'We'll be seen from the street else.'

The knowledge that he did not want to be seen either was something of a comfort. Anna followed him into the small room off the passage. He lit the candle again and closed the door. He was fat. Small, mud-coloured eyes were swamped by a pasty, baby's face. His hair was an eighth of an inch of fair stubble. He stared at her with interest.

Chapter 5

Anna looked around her. What she had taken to be a pile of mattresses was apparently a bed. A sleeping-bag lay on top, and there was an uncovered pillow propped against the wall.

'Do you sleep here?' she asked. 'Does Mr Marshall know?'

'He ain't been here for donkey's,' he said.

'Mrs Marshall?'

'She'd do her nut,' he admitted. 'But what can I do? Got to live somewhere, don't I? Me mum's old man gave me the boot, didn't he. Bastard.' He didn't look a day over twenty, Anna thought. And mercifully, he didn't look at all belligerent either. There was a frown line between his eyes which she associated with someone who is either constantly in pain or perpetually baffled. He didn't seem to be in pain. 'Look,' he went on worriedly. 'You shouldn't be here. There's nothing worth ripping off, believe me.'

'I'm not ripping anything off,' Anna said indignantly.

'Well, what then?'

'I'm looking for Edward Marshall.'

'Why?'

She had been lying her head off all day, and this didn't seem to be the right time to stop. She said, 'My sister's had the baby. He said he'd help if she kept quiet. Well, she's kept quiet but he seems to've scarpered. She's really strapped for cash now.'

'He's a bit of a lad, ennee?' he said with what sounded suspiciously like admiration.

'You're all alike,' Anna said bitterly. 'It may be a bit of fun to you but it can ruin some poor girl's whole life.' She was pleased to see that he looked instantly shamefaced. He said, 'Leave me out. I wouldn't do a thing like that.'

Not many women would let him, Anna thought. But she said softly, 'Yeah, sorry. But you can see the problem, can't you? It's not as if she's asking for much. sometimes I think just a kind word'd do. She's too unselfish for her own good, my sister. I really worry about her; she's so depressed. So I thought, you know, if I could just talk to him . . .'' She let the sentence trail off pathetically.

'I wish there was something I could do,' he said uncertainly.

'It's not like she wants to break up his marriage,' Anna went on, turning the screw a little tighter. 'He never told her he was married till after she fell pregnant, and then she felt so guilty she nearly topped herself.' She sighed. 'So I started asking around for him. But nobody's seen him.'

'Poor thing,' the fat boy said, looking sympathetic; whether because he felt sympathy or because he wanted to impress Anna, she couldn't tell. 'Honestly, if I knew where Mr Marshall was, I'd say, honest. But he bunged off last year and I ain't seen him since.'

'Where did he go?'

'Well, he goes off on these buying trips, see. Auctions,

house sales, you know. He said he was going down to Somerset.'

'Yeah?' Anna prompted.

'If you ask me, he's got someone on the side, down there,' he said, starting to leer before seeing Anna's expression and thinking better of it. 'Well, I mean, he always stays away ages on those trips and comes back all shagged out.'

'Have you ever been with him?' Anna asked.

'Not down there I ain't,' he told her. 'We went to Northampton once, and around the Midlands. But he always goes West on his tod. I think this time he's stayed shacked up with some bird. I mean, he's never been gone so long before.'

'Perhaps he owes someone money,' Anna suggested. 'I heard he tapped the sharks sometimes.'

'Could be,' he said. 'He likes to throw a big bundle around when he's flush. Though where he gets it beats me. He's not what you'd call a good businessman.'

'What do you do when he's away?'

'Well, the missus usually takes over, see. Only now the stock's all run down so she don't bother much. Me, I only work casual. He pays me by the day and there's other things I do. Suits me, this time anyway. Got a free kip, haven't I?'

'Oh well, looks like my sister'll have to be patient,' Anna said sadly. And then as an afterthought asked, 'What does he drive? I mean I could keep an eye out for his car if I knew what it was.'

'Green Sherpa,' he said. 'Nineteen-seventy-eight. It's got one grey panel at the back where someone shunted it.'

'License number?'

'Can't remember,' he said. 'Listen, if you see him, you won't mention me dossing here, will you?'

'Not if you don't mention me breaking in.' They grinned warily at each other. 'You'd better not tell his wife about my sister either,' Anna added.

'Not on your life,' he said, looking shocked. 'She's a right cow when she's got her back up.'

Anna left the way she had come. The fat boy couldn't find the key to the yard gate, but he gave her a leg-up over the fence instead. He seemed sorry to see her go and her last sight of him before she dropped back into the alley was standing with his arms dangling at his sides looking lonely as only a fat boy can.

In fact, she was very annoyed with herself. It had been stupid to break in, but it was cretinous to get caught. She was fairly sure that the fat boy wouldn't talk but she couldn't be certain and she hated to have her fate in someone else's hands. Most of all, her pride was wounded. It was bad enough to act unprofessionally but being witnessed was infinitely worse. And then, she had told a lot of stupid lies which she would have to remember for possible future reference. That was the trouble with lies: it was very important to remember them accurately when, generally, they were the things you most wanted to forget.

She went to bed in a fit of exasperation only to wake up feeling peevish. There were some things a good night's sleep did not improve. In this case it was because she would now have to concoct a story for Martin Brierly to explain what she now knew. Lies breed like rabbits, she thought, brushing her hair viciously.

She knew she was a good liar in that she was almost always believed, and sometimes she blamed her success on the gullibility of her victims. But this was like saying that

Marshall had encouraged her to break in by not having a safe lock on his door.

She comforted herself by remembering how many lies people told her. But then it was her job to ask questions; and if she asked more questions than most people it was only reasonable to expect more lies. The relation between the two was proportional. And, she reflected, she probably believed them as often as other people did. The only difference between herself and most others was that she was bound to test the information she received, so mostly she knew, after a while, when she had been lied to.

Chapter 6

Bernie said, 'Where's Frome?' looking up from his half-finished but meticulously handwritten report. He was the only member of Brierly Security who never used a typewriter. But, since his writing was quicker and neater than most of the others' typing, no one complained.

'Somerset,' Anna said. She hadn't known either until she had looked it up before going to bed last night. 'Not far from Bath.'

'Ah, Bath,' Bernie said, smiling as if something delightful had happened to him there. Anna, perched on the edge of his desk cradling a mug of tea, wondered what it was.

'Got anything planned for the weekend?' he went on.

'I'm supposed to take my nephew to Hamley's or somewhere, to choose a birthday present,' Anna said. 'And I want to strip down the carburetter. Why?'

'Well, only that if you tell the governor about Frome this morning, you'll likely be spending Saturday there rather than Hamley's.'

'That's a thought,' Anna said, frowning. 'No, that wouldn't do at all. The lad'd be awfully let down, and my sister'd give me stick for breach of promise.' The visit to Hamley's was an important annual event between Anna and her nephew. It was not so much the present that counted, rather the hours spent test-driving every suitable toy on show. Anna would never have admitted to anything so childish, but that was the part she enjoyed most too. She often thought that the visits must have been something of a calamity to the sales assistants. But they were the breath of life to Ken who had been brought up to look but not touch, almost as Anna herself had been. Not that he was either destructive or acquisitive. But he did like to be up to date on junior technology and he knew the value of experiment in such matters.

'Well then,' Bernie said, grinning at the look of consternation on her face. 'In that case, I wouldn't hang around here waiting for the old man, if I were you. It isn't urgent, is it? I mean, the mark's been gone for months, hasn't he?'

'Too right,' Anna said, making a grab for her coat. 'I hear Kilburn calling. What would I do without you thinking ahead for me?'

'Well, you might do it yourself,' he murmured gently to her retreating back.

There was not much she could usefully add to what she had already learned in Kilburn, but if she was going to strip the carburetter on Sunday, she would need the float chamber gasket. So she went straight to Drew's Auto Spares.

'It came in this morning,' the salesman said, sounding surprised: as if his written requests for items not in stock usually vanished without trace. Anna paid for the gasket and left the shop.

The Renault was parked on yellow lines across the road,

and a traffic warden who had just turned the corner about a hundred yards away was homing in on it like an Exocet. Anna dashed across the pavement trying to dodge a man who was making straight for Drew's. She sidestepped him quickly, and was just about to cross the road, when he pushed her from behind at the same time hooking her ankle with his foot.

She staggered forward and landed on hands and knees in the streaming gutter. A large brown suede shoe came down firmly on her hand.

'Upsy daisy,' the man said, kneeling down beside her but keeping his foot planted on her hand.

'Enjoy the trip, did you?' said someone else crouching on her other side. Anna recognized this one as Yellow Fang. She said, 'Get off my hand, you're crushing my fingers.'

'Me mate's ever so clumsy,' Yellow Fang said sympathetically. The mate moved his foot a fraction, but only to make the trap more secure. He said, 'Maybe you think you can kid Mrs Marshall, but if you're giving away free Aston Martins, I'm Miss Universe. Savvy?'

'Get your sodding foot off my hand and we'll talk,' Anna said through clenched teeth. Her fingers were throbbing unbearably.

'Be thankful he's only wearing his Hush Puppies,' Yellow Fang said amiably. 'What we mean is, stop hanging around the Marshalls. You're surplus to requirements, get it?'

Anna replied by sinking her teeth hard into the mate's knee. The weight on her hand lifted instantly and the mate sat down heavily in the gutter. 'The fucking bitch bit me!' he cried, outraged, as Anna scrambled to her feet.

Yellow Fang clamped a hand like a rat trap around her elbow. He held her stiff armed, away from him, so that she couldn't use her knees, and said, 'We could spoil those pretty pearlies for you, you know. One at a time. So be told. All right?'

Anna stared at him, but his face was completely without expression. He gave her elbow a violent twist and then let go.

She darted over the road to her car. Nobody stopped her. Her legs were shaking but she got in and drove off. The incident had hardly lasted a couple of minutes but there was already a parking ticket flapping under her windscreen-wiper. As she revved past Marshall's shop she saw that the 'Closed for Lunch' sign on the door was missing.

She rounded the corner, braked, and leaped out of the car. Looking apprehensively round the edge of the building, she saw Yellow Fang and his mate disappear at the other end of the street. They were a long way off, but Anna could have sworn they were laughing, and her pride hurt worse than her hand.

She loped quickly back to Marshall's shop, rubbing her fingers, and keeping a very sharp eye on the end of the street. They did not reappear so she opened the shop door and walked straight in.

If she had been unsure of Yellow Fang and his mate, there was no mistaking Jane Marshall. She was laughing her head off. She tired to stop when she saw Anna, but couldn't quite manage it.

'Your face!' she cried, breaking into shuddering gales of hilarity, 'when you found you couldn't get up. And his face when you bit his leg!' She doubled over, holding her sides. 'I could of died. I ain't seen nothing so funny since the Pink Panther.'

'Well, I'm glad it amused someone,' Anna said, offended. 'He could have broken my fingers.'

'It's your own silly fault,' Jane said, making another

attempt at self-control. 'That's all my eye about the car, ennit? You shouldn't go round raising people's hopes, should you? Oh my gawd, look at your jeans. You must of gone down on a load of dog crap. You don't half reek.' She collapsed into laughter again. 'And him with his wet bum. You should of seen the splash he made.'

'Who the hell are they, anyway?' Anna said angrily. There was indeed an evil-smelling smear on one knee of her jeans and the sight of it didn't improve her humour.

'None of your business,' Jane said, sobering up suddenly. 'You want to clear off and stay cleared off if you don't fancy no more nasty accidents.'

'Oh yeah?' Anna's temper, which had been fraying by the moment, snapped. 'Well, I'm not the one whose husband's gone missing. Laugh about that if you want something funny.'

'Oh, yeah?' Jane said, her eyes as narrow as cracks in the ceiling. 'Who says he's missing? Did I say he's missing?'

'Where is he, then?' Anna said. 'He's been gone since last September. Don't you want to know where he is?'

'What I want is you out of my shop,' Jane shouted. 'Go on, hop it, or I'll have the lads back.'

'All right,' Anna said, bitterly regretting her outburst. 'But I don't think you like the lads any more than I do. I think you're in trouble.'

'You come in here, up to your eyes in dog shit, and talk to me about trouble,' Jane yelled. 'Bugger off.'

'Okay,' Anna said, opening the door with as much dignity as she could muster. 'You've got my card. Ring, if you want help.'

'Look,' Jane said, advancing with menace in her eyes, 'I seen you on your knees in the gutter. And while you was down there, I seen a bleeding meter-maid give you an effing ticket. Would I come to you for help? Help's what you need, mate, not me.'

Anna drove home in a state of complete dejection. Apart from feeling humiliated, she was also quite puzzled. Jane did not know where Marshall was, she was sure of that from her reaction yesterday. But she did not want him found either. And then, she did not like her two protectors, but she seemed to rely on them. Anna tried to explain this to Martin Brierly later in the afternoon when, bathed and in clean clothes, she made her report.

'I think they must be either mob or cops,' she told him, after giving an expurgated version of her warning off. 'Nobody else behaves like that.'

'Please don't be facetious, Miss Lee,' Brierly snapped. 'I think I've already explained who they probably are. Now, if you'll be so good as to put your findings on paper, I will have something to show Mr Chivers when he calls in this evening. And be ready to drive to Somerset first thing on Monday morning. By then, no doubt, I will have ascertained whether or not Mr Thurman wishes to pursue this case out of town.'

Chapter 7

The weekend had sped by, giving Anna little time for reflection. Now she was driving west on the M4. The carburetter seemed fine, and it was not until after the Membury Service Station, when she met a strong west wind head on, that the little Renault began to struggle. But by now the hills were rolling and green and, even though she had to keep her foot hard on the accelerator to maintain even sixty miles an hour, she enjoyed the drive.

Frome was a market town. It was neither pretty nor ugly and it looked well used. A stone cross stood in the old market place which was nothing more than a widening of the main road where four banks and a hotel squared up to each other.

Anna parked near the cross and went on foot to look for the post office. It was not far, but it was so crowded that she decided to ask for directions elsewhere. It was only when she had been given directions that she realized she would need a map to make sense of them. And when she had found the map, she decided that she couldn't make sense of that either without a good lunch under her belt.

Lunch was a wonderful old-fashioned kedgeree eaten in a dauntingly old-fashioned coffee shop. While she was eating, she discovered from the map that, although she had understood North Parade, The Bridge, Market Place and Bath Street to be four separate roads, they were, in fact, all one. With this knowledge her instruction became simple. But it showed up an annoying fact of life: working away from home was a confusing, lengthy business.

Bailing and Sparrow was housed in a terrace of old buildings of wildly differing styles and dates. A colourful display board advertised properties for sale but there the connection with the twentieth century ended. The outer office was decorated with dark cream and brown paint and the desks were solid, time-blackened oak.

A slim girl with Rossetti hair greeted Anna from behind one of the outsized desks.

Anna explained that she was trying to trace a missing person who might have been to one of Bailing and Sparrow's auctions last October. Had the auction taken place, and if so, could anyone tell her if Marshall had attended?

The girl was intrigued by the inquiry. She looked up the firm's records and said that the auction had been held on October 5th. It had taken place in a private house. If Marshall had bought anything, she said, his name would appear on the sales lists. What happened, she explained, was that a successful bidder for any item had his name written on the list next to the number of the lot he had bid for. These lists were then passed on to the cashier who made out a proper receipt when the items were paid for later.

The girl disappeared into a back room and, after a long

pause, came back with the lists for October 5th. Both she and Anna poured over them but, after checking each page twice, had to agree that Marshall's name was not there.

'That only means that he didn't buy anything,' the girl said. 'He could have been there.'

Anna agreed and produced Marshall's photograph. The girl did not recognize him, but, as she said, she was only office staff. She hardly ever went to auctions. 'You might try Stan Ridge,' she suggested. 'He's the one who deals most with the buyers. If your Mr Marshall's in the trade, he probably comes regularly and Stan might know him.'

Stan Ridge was out that afternoon pricing some farm equipment. The girl couldn't tell when he would be finished. 'Where are you staying?' she asked, 'I'll ask him to give you a call when he gets back.'

This brought up another problem. Anna had been hoping to finish that day and be home by the same night. Although she had packed a bag, just in case, she had not booked into a hotel.

'You could try The Mendip Hills,' the girl suggested. 'It's only a little way out of town, but it's quiet and has modern bathrooms.'

Anna thanked her sincerely for the trouble she had taken and went off to find The Mendip Hills. She checked in and found it to be an average, mid-priced commercial hotel: the sort that Beryl would not kick up a fuss about when she saw the bill.

That done, Anna drove to Galvin, Cox and Ross which was on the other side of Frome.

The offices were attached to a warehouse which served as an auction room. Billboards on the warehouse doors told her the dates of the next five sales, but as nothing was going on that Monday Anna went directly into the office.

One glance at the secretary in the front office told her how lucky she had been with the girl with Rossetti hair. This one was round-shouldered, dull-eyed and had a streaming cold. A small plaque on her desk said, Miss P. Vobster, Sec.

Anna explained her business and asked to see the sales lists for September 29th. Miss P. Vobster, Sec. coughed noisily and said, 'Sorry, but Mr Cox is out just now.'

'It isn't Mr Cox I want to see,' Anna said, stepping out of range of flying bacilli. 'Just the sales lists.'

'Mr Cox is our chief auctioneer,' Miss Vobster informed her. 'He handles all sales inquiries.'

'Is there someone else I could talk to?' Anna asked. 'For instance, who goes round during an auction taking the names of the buyers?'

'Well, there's Adam, I suppose,'' Miss Vobster said, pausing to spray her appointments diary with a massive sneeze. 'He's in the yard checking a delivery.'

Adam, in fact, wasn't checking anything. He was sitting on the tailboard of a large truck, dragging deeply on a cigarette and listening to Radio One.

'You from London?' he said, when Anna had gone through her story again. 'I've got friends there. You can have a good time in London, not like here.'

'Yes,' Anna said patiently. 'Edward Marshall's from London too. Perhaps you know him?' She flourished the photograph. Adam took it and laughed. He said, 'Oh yeah, Fast Eddie. I know him. He comes here every now and then.'

'Great, ' Anna said eagerly. 'Did he come last September?'

'How would I remember that?' Adam said. 'But I do

remember him. One time he came in the pub I go to and pulled my mate's girlfriend right from under his nose.'

'When was that?'

'I don't know, sometime last year. he's not exactly welcome at my pub any more. My mate still wants his guts for garters.'

'But you're the one who takes the name of anyone who buys something in the auctions,' Anna persisted. 'So, if anyone knew if he was here in September, it'd be you.'

'I suppose I could look,' he said unwilllingly. 'The books are kept in the office.'

'They'd be very kind,' Anna wheedled.

He came back after about ten minutes looking irritated. 'That Penny's a lazy cow,' he complained. 'She didn't want to let me have the key. But I got it in the end. Your Fast Eddie was here on the twenty-ninth. He bought four wheel-backed chairs and a small pine chest. All right?'

'Terrific,' Anna said. 'Where would he stay in Frome and what would he do with the goods he bought?'

'Well, after he'd paid, he'd just load them up and be on his way. I've no idea where he'd stay. Some people stop at The Railway Bridge Hotel, or there's The Crown or The Mendip Hills. But some just camp in their lorries, and there's others with regular lodgings. They come from all over, you know.'

'Well, thanks anyway,' Anna said, getting ready to leave. 'By the way, does your friend's girl still see him?'

'Nah,' Adam said, looking contemptuous. 'He's just here today, gone tomorrow. She ought to've known better.'

Chapter 8

Anna stopped at The Railway Bridge and she stopped at The Crown. She also stopped at any place with a Bed and Breakfast sign in between, but nobody knew Edward Marshall and nobody recognized his photograph. That left The Mendip Hills, so she went back there and, while collecting her room key, showed the photograph to the man at the reception desk. He was young and looked as if he had studied hotel management at evening classes. He did not recognize the picture but looked up the dates between September 28th and October 5th in the register. There was no trace there either.

Anna went to her room and telephoned the office. Beryl said, 'Where are you staying? What do they charge?' Anna told her. Account books were more important to Beryl than case files. She also reported progress so far and said she hoped to be back the next day.

'Good,' Beryl said waspishly. 'We don't want you running round the countryside, wasting the firm's resources. And remember, I won't pay for anything I don't see a proper receipt for.'

After being so tactfully reminded, Anna jotted down her expenses so far and clipped all the receipts together. The telephone rang, and a strange voice said, 'This is Stanley Ridge from Bailing and Sparrow. Miss Henry told me you'd like a word.'

Wonderful Miss Henry, Anna thought. 'Yes,' she said. 'Would you like to have a drink here?'

'Fine,' he said. 'We'll meet in the bar. I'll be about thirty-five minutes.'

The bar was standard twentieth-century Tudor with candles in glass jars on the tables. What she could see of Stan Ridge looked pleasant enough so she smiled and ordered him a Scotch and water.

He said, 'Miss Henry told me you were inquiring after a chap called Edward Marshall. I didn't remember the name so I looked back through our records for this year and last year. It appears in February and June last year, but that's all. He doesn't seem to be a big spender, but he is on our current mailing list.'

'It's very good of you to take so much trouble,' Anna said, thinking that Bailing and Sparrow were very lucky to employ two such helpful people. 'I'd be very interested to know if you saw him at your sale on October the fifth.' A waitress came over with the drinks and swished her skirt at Stan Ridge. Anna couldn't really blame her as he was the only man under sixty in the bar that evening.

He said, 'Miss Henry told me you had a photo. Cheers.'

'Cheers,' Anna replied, giving him the picture. He studied it carefully in the candlelight and then said, 'Yes, I do know the face. He's trade all right, but I can't say if I saw him in October. It's just too long ago to remember properly.'

'Never mind,' Anna said, disappointed. 'How about this year?'

'I don't know,' he said regretfully. 'I might have. But you know this is a common type of face round here. Lots of chaps look like this.' He flicked the photograph lightly with his fingernails to indicate the sideburns. 'Of a certain sort,' he added discreetly.

'I think he came from the Midlands originally,' Anna said, wondering for the first time if this was really so. All Mr Thurman had said was that he had met him in Birmingham. His wife was a Londoner. There was no doubt about her. Not that it mattered really.

'It must be interesting work you do,' Stan Ridge suggested hopefully. Anna sighed and ordered more drinks. They chatted politely about private investigators and the auction trade until Stan looked at his watch and said he had a dinner date.

Anna stayed in the bar finishing her lager and thinking. If she left now, she could probably be home by ten. On the other hand, the room was paid for so she might as well use it. She was quite tired and wouldn't have minded an early night, but she didn't sleep very well in hotel rooms; there was always something wrong with the ventilation.

The waitress came to collect the glasses. She said cosily, 'Good-looking, ennee? Friend of yours, is he?'

'The bloke who just left?' Anna said, surprised. 'I only just met him.'

'Not him.' The waitress giggled. 'He.' She pointed emphatically at the photo.

'Why?' Anna asked, suddenly alert. 'Do you know him?'

'I might do,' the waitress said coyly. 'If he's the same one as walked out with Kirsty. Looks like him. What's his name?'' Anna told her and she giggled again. 'Sounds like him too.'

'Who's Kirsty?' Anna asked. 'Sit down for a minute.'

'I couldn't.' The waitress looked over her shoulder at the barman. 'I'll take the snap though and show it to Kirsty. She's on kitchen duty tonight.'

She was gone for about ten minutes. When she returned, she gave back the picture and said excitedly, 'It is him. I knew it. Kirsty wants to see you. Will you? She's ever so upset.' She was pink-faced with enjoyment. It looked as if this was the biggest thrill she'd had in a month of Sundays.

'Okay,' Anna said. 'Where?'

'Go to the staff toilets,' the waitress said. 'Next to the kitchen. I'll show you where. You'll have to hurry, though. The chef's ever so mean.'

They waited until the barman was concentrating on a group of customers and then Anna followed her out and along a passage that led to the kitchen.

Anna's acquaintance with Jane Marshall had led her to suppose that Edward's taste was for big, tough women so Kirsty was a surprise to her. She was tiny. The white overalls and hairband made her look immature and childish.

'This is Kirsty,' the waitress whispered loudly. 'I'll keep a lookout, shall I?'

'Don't bother,' Kirsty said in a low voice. 'I'm sorry, but I promise I'll tell you everything later.'

The waitress tiptoed away looking bitterly disappointed.

'She's a terrible gossip,' Kirsty said, watching the cloakroom door swing. 'But she means well, I suppose.' She took a deep breath and said, 'Is Eddie your husband?'

'Good grief no,' Anna said, aghast.

'But I thought that's why you came,' Kirsty said, looking equally surprised. 'I thought you was his wife and you was looking for evidence to divorce him with. He never said, but I know in my heart of hearts he was wed.'

'Well, he is, I'm afraid,' Anna said, 'but not to me.'

'That's a relief,' Kirsty muttered. There were tears in her eyes. 'I don't know what I was going to say if you was his wife. I feel that ashamed.'

'It's not your fault, if he didn't tell you.'

Kirsty shook her head. 'I didn't ask, neither. And I should've. I just hoped, see.' She wiped her eyes with the back of her hand. The knuckles were red and chapped.

'Why don't you tell me about it?' Anna asked softly.

'Oh, I can't stop,' Kirsty said looking up, wide-eyed. 'I'm only supposed to've gone to wash my hands.'

'Well, come to my room when you get off work. I'm in Room forty-three.'

'It'll be awfully late,' she said unwillingly, 'and my mum worries.'

'Please come,' Anna said urgently. 'It's important.'

'All right,' Kirsty said, after a moment's hesitation. 'Only I've got to go now.'

It wasn't only the kitchen staff the chef used a heavy hand on, Anna thought, as she toiled through overdone steak and chips. The menu promised much but what it delivered was badly cooked, tough, and late. Afterwards, she avoided the bar and went up to her room to watch television and wait for Kirsty. She wished she had brought a book.

It was nearly midnight when Kirsty tapped on the door. She sat on the end of the bed with her hands in her lap looking, if possible, even more childish than before. Her clothes were all a size too big, as if she were still expecting to grow into them.

'Can I see the photo again?' she asked timidly. It obviously gave her pain, but Anna suspected she was enjoying herself too. After waiting respectfully for a few minutes, Anna said, 'You were going to tell me about him.'

'There's nothing to tell, really,' Kirsty said, with a light in her eyes that said something different. 'We went out when he was here, but months'd go by when I never saw him. I always waited for him, though. I never minded waiting.'

She saw herself as the heroine of a romantic story, Anna decided: the faithful bride watching the water or some such rubbish. It would probably be mostly true, if she left out the dramatic bits.

'In the summer,' Kirsty went on, 'we went down by the river and talked. It was lovely.'

'What about now?' Anna coaxed.

'There is no now,' Kirsty said with simple pathos. 'He left me.'

'Oh, well, bad luck,' Anna mumbled clumsily. 'When was that?'

'When I walked in the pub,' she said slowly, 'I saw them together. She had her hand on his knee, and I knew it was all over. He said he was sorry and I was too good for him. It didn't do her no good, neither,' she added in a more down to earth tone of voice. 'She hasn't seen him since last autumn. She had to come round my mum's back door asking me if I'd taken him back.'

'Who is she?'

'Charlene Cooper. She didn't wait, though,' she said scornfully. 'She went to London with a man from the Electricity Board. I think they're married now.'

'Why don't you go to London too?' Anna said, on an impulse. There was something very claustrophobic about the thought of Kirsty in a hotel kitchen, waiting endlessly for the one creep who had brought some romance into her life. She sat passively on the end of Anna's bed like a small jug waiting to have life poured into it. She said proudly, 'Oh, I couldn't. I haven't even had a holiday since he left. You see, we met down at the kitchen door, and if he comes back he'll look for me there.' She had obviously decided on a career of martyrdom, Anna thought, half impatient, half sorry for her. She said, 'What on earth was he doing at the kitchen door?'

'Selling something,' Kirsty said mysteriously.

'Selling furniture in a hotel kitchen?' Anna asked, perplexed.

'No, silly. Meat. It's his sideline.'

'Meat?' Anna was really puzzled now. 'How does a bloke in the furniture trade get to be a butcher in his spare time?'

'Not a butcher,' Kirsty said, offended. 'A huntsman.'

'I don't understand,' Anna said truthfully: the conversation had skidded off the road somewhere.

'Well, sometimes he brought pheasant,' Kirsty said patiently, 'but mostly it was venison.'

'He was a poacher?' Light dawned.

'That's what they said.' Kirsty looked insulted. 'Actually, it's survival off the land. Wild animals are nobody's property.' She was quoting, Anna thought. She said quickly, 'Sorry. Who else called him a poacher?'

'There was some trouble,' Kirsty admitted, 'and the chef lost his job.'

'What happened?'

Kirsty folded her tiny lips stubbornly and looked down at her hands.

'Well, never mind,'' Anna said hurriedly. She had a sudden insight into what might have happened, and if it was correct, the last person to tell her about it was Kirsty. 'Did the chef get another job?'

He had moved to Bath, Anna found out, to work at an Italian restaurant called Vito's. Kirsty seemed very pleased at his demotion. After a little more digging, Anna got his name too. That would have to do for the present. Kirsty was extremely reluctant to talk any more and went away soon afterwards, sliding quietly out of Anna's room. A small, empty person living a small, empty life, Anna thought, brushing her teeth and feeling obscurely depressed.

Chapter 9

Bath was the sort of self-consciously beautiful town where the antique shops outnumber the pubs. What Anna liked about it was the toast-and-honey-coloured stone it was built with. There was even a flash or two of sun to bring out the colour.

Vito's was closed until eleven, so Anna went to look at the Royal Crescent instead. It yawned like a condescending smile from across a well-trimmed green, and even so early in the year, there were plenty of tourists paying homage with clicking cameras. It was obviously a town you were supposed to walk in, Anna decided when she had failed to find anywhere to have the Renault. In the end she saw quite a lot of Bath and wasted even more time simply looking for a car park. It was too elegant a place to have car parks where they were needed.

Even so, Vito's was still closed when she got back there. But she found the man she was looking for unloading crates of fruit and lettuces from a greengrocer's van. As the manager had not arrived, he took her down to the kitchen for a cup of tea.

'None of that foaming eye-tie cappocheenee for me,' he remarked, handing her a cup of dark brown brew strong enough to coat the teeth. The kitchen was small and dark and the memory of chopped onions clung to the walls like paint. 'You don't have to be Italian to cook Italian food,' he told her amiably. 'Just slap on the old garlic and they never know the difference.'

Anna made a mental note never to eat upstairs. He was a careless, good-natured man of about forty and she found him easy to talk to.

'Eddie's one of nature's capitalists,' he said about the poaching. 'Shows a bit of enterprise; does everyone a favour. Cheap game, that's all it was. Everyone in the hotel business is at it. The management turns a blind eye. Everyone happy. Of course, when that silly little moo shopped us, they had to sit up and take notice.'

'Kirsty shopped you?' Anna asked, although it was what she had expected.

'Poor little cow,' he said tolerantly. 'She thought she'd been betrayed so she had to get even. Anyone with half an eye could see Eddie wasn't really interested anyway. Leching girls is just a habit with him. But she had to take him serious. Some of these kids never learn.'

When Anna asked where Eddie was now, he said, 'I haven't seen any of them again. We don't serve game in this dump.' He chuckled and added, 'Tortelloni Deery Mio, can you imagine it?'

'Any of them?' Anna asked. ''Does Eddie have friends down here?'

'Course he does. He's one of the lads is our Eddie,' he said, winking. But he would not say who the other lads were. 'I know you're not the law,' he explained. 'But all the same I don't think they'd like me giving out names and addresses. Eddie's got some form back in London. Well, you'd know that already if you know anything about him at all. So I'll just leave it at that. Nothing personal, mind.' As he wouldn't be budged, Anna gave him her business card and asked him to get in touch if he changed his mind.

She drove back to The Mendip Hills. Edward Marshall was turning out to be a complicated sort of man: furniture dealer, fraud, poacher, husband, con and lech. One of nature's capitalists, indeed. She wondered what else he might be and, more important, where?

She booked her room for another night and then asked the young man with the business school manners about the incident in the kitchen.

'Oh, that Edward Marshall,' he said, looking as if she had put something that smelled nasty under his nose. 'I thought you were trying to locate a guest. Most unpleasant, really. It's a bit like receiving stolen goods,' he added primly. 'If the story had got out it would have been most embarrassing for the hotel. And on top of that, the chef was putting in enormous bills for the meat, but only paying a fraction of that to the poachers. When we found that out we had no choice but to let him go.'

A slightly different version of the chef's story, Anna noticed. She asked, 'Was Edward Marshall prosecuted?'

'Good heavens no. We didn't want any publicity. Mind you,' he went on in a lower voice, 'there were some parties rather disappointed we wouldn't.'

'Who?'

'Well, old Donald Parrish in particular. He's the stalker for some of the estates just north of here. He caught one of them. But we couldn't cut our own throats for him, now could we?'

He couldn't tell her where to find Donald Parrish, so she looked him up in the directory and discovered that he lived in a place called Freezing Hill. The manager showed her where it was on the map though, and wished her luck.

Anna ran up to her room and made a quick call to London to ask Beryl to make some inquiries about Marshall's police record.

'We were expecting you back this morning,' Beryl grumbled. 'Don't get too comfy down there. That hotel isn't cheap, you know.'

Freezing Hill was no colder than anywhere else that day. Donald Parrish had a cottage near the top overlooking acres of pine and beech forest. Anna knocked at the front door, but there was no reply. In fact it looked as if the front door was rarely used so she went round to the back.

There were two pens in the yard, with hens in one and three dogs in the other. They all set up such a clamour of combined barking and clucking that she had no need to knock, and after a while an old woman in a brilliant red and blue flowered apron appeared to see who was being murdered.

'Is Mr Parrish at home?' Anna asked, while the three dogs bounced hysterically off the wire walls of their pen behind her.

'What?' said the old woman, and Anna saw her deaf-aid hanging by its wire from the top pocket of her dress.

'Mr Parrish,' she shouted again, pointing to the useless deaf-aid.

'Battery's dead,' the woman said gently. 'What was it you wanted?'

'Mr Parrish,' yelled Anna, and the dogs yelled back, demented with fury.

'I'm Mrs Parrish.'

'Your husband,' Anna shouted at the top of her voice. No wonder the poor woman was deaf if she had to put up with this racket every time anyone came to the door.

'Oh,' Mrs Parrish said. 'He'll be home at half past five for his tea. Come back at about half past six.'

Anna nodded and smiled and drove back to Frome with her ears ringing.

Chapter 10

The wind was up and sending dark-bottomed clouds rocketing across the sky over Freezing Hill. The trees bent their backs under its weight and Anna turned up her collar and walked into the stalker's yard to face the combined fury of dogs and chickens again.

He came out of his house, stooping under the lintel. He was not a cottage-sized man. First he roared, 'Sharrup, y'buggers,' at the dogs, who instantly left off snarling and pounding the wire with their bodies and sat, tongues lolling, like ordinary domestic pooches. Anna quite expected the wind to die at his command too.

He extended a vast red hand that looked like a rubber glove and said, 'My wife said you'd be calling. What can I do for you?'

Anna introduced herself and explained, 'I'm looking for a man called Edward Marshall. I was told at the hotel that you caught him or one of his friends round here last autumn.' She produced the photograph and he put on a pair of steel-rimmed spectacles to study it. He took his time. Then he said, 'Oh yes,' and gave the picture back without any other comment.

Anna said, 'I wonder if you could tell me about him.' She was a little intimidated by him: he was so big and quiet, and he stood so solidly while the wind raged around him scarcely ruffling his curly white hair, while she felt as substantial as tissue paper. From the thick leather boots on his feet to the cord jacket with leather patches that cased his wide shoulders, he was dressed entirely in various shades of brown.

He took off his glasses and said, 'Well, I was just going out again. You can either wait here or come along. I shouldn't be more than an hour.'

Anna was always willing to try anything once, so she said she'd come too. He flicked his eyes over her thin jacket and jeans and grinned briefly.

He went back indoors and appeared again shortly wearing a bulky waterproof, a hat, and carrying a rifle. He went over to the pen and unlatched the gate, holding it a few inches ajar so that the terrier, who was smaller and quicker than the others, could wriggle out. He shut it quickly as the two Labradors pressed forward whining their disappointment. The terrier, shrill with joy, set off, nose to the ground, round the yard like a high speed vacuum cleaner.

Mr Parrish's truck was splattered to the windows with mud. Anna got in and found that the interior was in much the same state. The terrier was tossed unceremoniously into the back. Mr Parrish clipped his rifle to a gunrack behind his head and they set off, bumping out of the yard and on to the road.

At length he said, 'One of the estate managers phoned just now and said he saw a lame buck over the other side of the hill. That's where we're going now.'

'If you find it, do you have to shoot it?' Anna asked. 'Is that what a stalker does?'

'One of the things,' he said, peering through the windscreen. 'You'd get rid of a wounded buck, of course.' The light was fading but he did not turn on his headlamps. 'There's too many of them about anyway. We get complaints from the farmers round here. See, the deer leave the woods at night and come out to graze on farmland.' He swung the truck into a small turning and stopped in front of a gate. Anna got out, opened it and waited for him to drive through before shutting it.

'Look there,' he said, when she was sitting beside him again. There were two fields of grass which ended abruptly where a black wall of fir trees began. 'That's where your poacher likes to go. They come after dark and drive on to the field. They turn on the headlights, see, and catch the buck in the high beam. The buck stands stock still, blinded, see.'

'And gets shot?' Anna asked, looking out over the darkening green grass.

'Sometimes, but you'd hear a shot for miles out here. No, they use dogs, Lurchers, most like, to bring the deer down. The poacher cuts its throat. Simple.'

'One dog can bring down a deer?' Anna said incredulously, her mind on packs of hounds and antlered stag.

'You've never seen Roe Deer?' he asked, smiling. 'They don't come no more than thirty inches high. it's your Red Deer that grow to any size.'

'Oh,' she said, feeling stupid. 'And that's what you caught Edward Marshall doing?'

He put the truck into gear and drove slowly over the track between the fields towards the wood. 'Not that, no. Least-ways, I didn't see no dogs. It wasn't here, neither. But somewhere like. I got a call, see. Someone'd seen vehicles as didn't belong on the estate. Everyone keeps an eye out, see. Especially September, October when the pheasants are grown. Well, I found the cars. Car and a van, it was.'

The truck was suddenly swallowed by the wood and they started downhill between even ranks of pinetrees. The light was dim and grey.

'I waited till I saw movement over t'other side of the field,' he went on. 'And then I circled round and came up behind them. There was four. At least, I only saw four. So I grabbed the nearest.'

'And the others legged it?'

'Like rabbits,' he agreed. 'Anyway, I had the one, and I shone my torch in his face so I'd know who he was. Poachers're local men, mostly. But he was a stranger. Told me his name was John Wayne.' He laughed. 'Oh, the things they do say when you've got them by the collar! Well, coming across the field, we had a bit of a tussle and he hopped it. There's not much I can do, see. As it was, he couldn've sued me for assault. A stalker don't even have the rights a gamekeeper do. Silly, really, but there 'tis. Still, I had their licence numbers. So I reported it.'

'Couldn't you've called the police before you went after them?' Anna asked. 'And gone there with them?' They were driving through a patch of beech forest now and the light was better.

'Oh, I call them, right enough,' he said with his gruff laugh. 'But sometimes they're as far away as Warminster or Devizes. Your poacher don't hang about forever.'

He braked gently, and they came to a stop in a clearing where two more tracks met the one they were on.

'You want to see Roe Deer?' he asked quietly. 'There's one

at the top of that bank there.' He pointed and Anna looked along his arm. The trunks of the beeches were smooth and grey-green with algae; the ground covered with russet leaves from last autumn. No grass grew underneath. She stared where he was pointing, but she couldn't see a thing.

'Where?' she said at last, thinking he might be having her on.

'There. About sixty yards off, and about five foot left of that little clump of saplings.'

If it hadn't moved, she would never have seen it. But just then it lifted its head and stepped daintily away behind the saplings, brown on the back, pale fawn on the belly, neat white rump twitching. The feet, she thought, would hardly fill an eggcup.

'They're prettier, come summer,' he said, putting the car in gear. 'All red gold. But by then she'll've dropped her kids. That's a fair sight, too.'

How a man who needed spectacles to see a photograph could know that the tiny creature was female, let alone a pregnant one, she couldn't imagine.

'She wasn't lame, was she?' Anna asked, afraid that her first Roe Deer would soon be deceased.

'Course not,' he said, giving her a sideways glance of mingled amusement and scorn. He started the truck and they wound their way slowly down the hill.

'So, what did the police do?' Anna said, hoping to lead the conversation back to more familiar territory.

'Well, about then, there'd been this bit of fuss at the hotel. So the police already had their eyes out for your Marshall. They stopped his van that very night and pulled him in. Well, of course, if he'd had any carcases in the van, he'd got rid of them long since. And they never found his knife neither.'

'What knife?'

'When I had him, he had this girt big thing. American it is. What they do call a Bowie. But he must've left it somewhere. So he says, "Well, Officer, I was just out for a breath of fresh air," see, "when this bloody big hooligan jumps on my back." That's me, in case you don't recognize the description. He says, "There's no law against taking a break of fresh air, is there?"'

'It's wonderful what they do think of,' he went on. 'You can catch them kneeling by the carcase, their knives red and dripping, but when they come up before the magistrate, it's all "Oh sorry, your Honour, but I was just taking my doggie for a walk when I came upon this poor wounded deer. I just had to put it out of its misery, didn't I? Can't stand to see a poor animal suffer." Fair makes your heart bleed, don't it?'

Anna had to laugh. She said, 'So I suppose they let him go, did they?'

He shrugged. 'If those mealy-mouthed hotel people had owned up to buying venison from him, we'd've been away. But of course they wouldn't.' he stopped the truck again and opened the door. When he had unclipped his gun and lifted the terrier out of the back, he said, 'I shan't be long. You can come with me or stay in the truck if you'd rather. Please yourself.'

Anna followed him along a narrow footpath between the trees. It was about an hour before sunset, she reckoned, but not much daylight found its way below the pine canopy. High above, the wind ripped noisily through the tree-tops.

Mr Parrish looked as if he was walking normally, but he hardly made a sound. Anna who knew she must be at least five stone lighter, crashed around like a football team, and was very embarrassed at the racket she was making. She tried to watch where she put her feet but somehow always managed to smash a dry twig or kick a stone.

They came to a large clearing. It was mostly taken up by an enclosure of wire netting. An electric fence ran around the perimeter about a foot from the ground. The enclosure was empty except for the nettles, grass and new bracken that couldn't grow under the thick cover of the forest. From the branches of the surrounding trees hung the grizzly remains of long dead crows and nearer the ground Anna caught the gleam of dozens of dull lights. Looking more closely she saw that these were lazily revolving shards of broken mirror suspended by string from the branches.

'Pheasant pen,' Mr Parrish explained shortly, skirting round the edge. 'The gamekeepers do say the moonlight on the glass scares the owls and foxes.'

Anna couldn't speak for the owls, but the sight of the dangling mirrors and rotten crows made her skin come up in goose bumps. It looked more like the site of some pre-Christian ritual than a nursery for young birds.

The next clearing was much bigger and had been made by foresters. On the edge were piles of sawn tree-trunks waiting to be carted away. The ground was scarred back to the clay by the wheels of heavy machinery.

Mr Parrish showed Anna a rough platform, about eighteen feet high, half-hidden by the trees. A ladder led to the top. She climbed up and he followed. The terrier was nowhere to be seen.

'Sit still and wait,' he said, laying the gun between them close to his right hand. The hide caught the full force of the wind, rocking slightly with the gusts, and slowly Anna felt herself stiffening with the cold. She thought she saw moving shapes everywhere but what she took for deer always turned out to be a log or a stump. She almost shivered with suspense waiting for the shot that would kill the lame buck.

After a while Mr Parrish said, 'They may not come out in the open with all this wind. When 'tis noisy like this they likes to stay under cover.' But after another ten minutes he said, 'Wait a bit. Over there, see?'

Anna strained her eyes in the gloom but she saw nothing. He said, 'You must see them. There's three together, moving just in the edge of the wood there.'

She could see the woods, and she could see the bushes between the trees, but for the life of her she could not see anything moving. He raised his rifle and squinted through the scope.

'Any lame ones?' Anna whispered.

'Not they,' he said, putting the gun down again.

They stayed until Mr Parrish said it was too dark for him to see. As this was nearly a quarter of an hour after Anna had started crediting him with infra-red eyes, she was quite relieved. He had pointed out deer on three other occasions but she hadn't seen any of them.

Donald Parrish four, Anna Lee nil, she thought stumbling after him in the dark, her feet and hands numb with cold.

In the truck, he kindly switched on the heater for her and turned for home. She asked him if he had recognized any of Edward Marshall's companions, but he said he hadn't. Nor did he know if the police had checked on the number of the second car.

When they arrived back at his cottage, he told her she had done quite well for a novice. 'At least you didn't spend all your time complaining like most of the city ladies,' he said with a broad grin. 'You should come out with me sometime when the weather's better. You'll be a good shot, I suppose.'

'Who, me?' Anna said, startled. 'I've hardly ever used a rifle in my life.'

'I thought all you detectives were crack shots,' he said, his eyes twinkling innocently. Anna couldn't be quite sure, not being used to the accent, but she thought he pronounced it 'defectives' and 'crap shots'.

Half an hour later she stepped thankfully into a deep, hot bath at The Mendip Hills, and soaked the chill out of her bones.

Chapter 11

She was still soaking when the telephone rang. It had to be Beryl, she thought, struggling out of the bath and winding a towel around herself. No one else had such an unerring instinct for inconvenient moments, except perhaps Selwyn.

'Why don't you keep in touch?' Beryl said, the telephone line making her voice even thinner and more irritable than usual. 'What on earth have you been doing? I've been ringing every half-hour since six o'clock.'

'For your information, ' Anna replied crossly, 'I spent the morning in Bath, the afternoon in Frome and the evening in the freezer. And I've discovered that our Mr Marshall is not only a con-artist, but also a poacher who's's been run in by the local fuzz at least once. I'll be seeing them tomorrow. Then I'm coming home.'

'No you're not,' Beryl said smugly. 'Tomorrow you're going to Quarmeford.'

'What for?' Anna protested. 'Look, Beryl, I'm cold and

tired and I've just discovered I'm not too brilliant in the country. Can't the old man send someone else?'

'Too bad,' Beryl said. 'You're already there. Now stop kidding around and listen to me. I received a phone call this afternoon from someone who claims to know where Edward Marshall is. The Commander and I have replayed the tape several times and we're agreed that it's genuine.'

'Oh, jolly good,' Anna exclaimed. 'What if I don't agree it's genuine? Where the hell is Quarmeford anyway?'

'On Exmoor,' Beryl said briskly. 'Now, this person will meet you somewhere on the road between Quarmeford and Porlock at two o'clock tomorrow afternoon. The instructions are quite precise so you shouldn't have any trouble finding him.'

'Who am I supposed to be meeting?'

'Ah, well, he didn't leave his name,' Beryl said. 'But I spoke to him at length and the Commander agrees that he sounds like a responsible man.'

'He sounds like a responsible man?' Anna asked flatly. 'Look, Beryl, this isn't like meeting some punter outside Marks and Spencer, you know.'

Beryl sighed loudly and said, 'Stop being so imaginative and listen. Have you got a pencil? You leave Quarmeford on the Porlock Road. The road forks after two miles. Three and a quarter miles further on . . . are you listening, Anna? Three and a quarter miles . . . got that? Right, well on the left-hand side of the road you'll see a lay-by. It's quite distinctive because there's a hawthorn tree growing there and it's the only one for miles around. Stop there. Get out of the car and climb up on top of the bank where you can be seen . . . What? I don't know what bank. You'll see it when you get there. And incidentally what do you mean by wasting my time asking about Marshall's record? He hasn't got one. CRO were very shirty about it. There's goodwill involved, you know, and I don't want to fritter it away on frivolities.'

Coming from anyone else, the meeting on the moor would have been exciting news. But Beryl had a unique talent for making the politest instruction sound like an imposition.

By morning, Anna had forgotten her annoyance and set out early. It was a long drive and she wanted to get to the meeting place well ahead of time so that she could have a good look around first.

As it was, she miscalculated. A lot of time was wasted behind slow-moving farm machinery on narrow, winding roads and she arrived with only ten minutes to spare.

She had crawled up the steep hill from Quarmeford in second gear on a lane sunk like a moat between banks of beech hedge. On top of the hill the moor rose suddenly like the back of a surfacing whale and the heavy grey sky seemed to reach down to meet it.

The road cut its way uncertainly between a rise on one side and a dip on the other. Anna found the place easily after three and a quarter miles of what looked like senseless meandering. The hawthorn was old and knotted and leaned drunkenly away from the wind. She supposed it was a hawthorn, but it sported neither flower nor leaf. Spring was naturally reluctant to show itself in such an exposed place.

She got out and locked the car: city habit. Silly habit here, when, as far as the eye could see, there was no one around for miles. She climbed the bank and was hit hard by a wind which raked the moor from the direction of the sea. Like the hawthorn, she turned her back on it.

There was no one waiting for her. A few black-faced sheep turned and looked at her, their wool hanging in tatters from lean and muscular bodies. They were nothing like the roly-poly creatures that trundled languidly over lowland grass.

She took her binoculars out of their case. Through the glasses she could see fold upon fold of hill and valley. It would probably be lovely with the heather in flower and the bracken at its height. Now, the bracken only came to knee level, just beginning to uncurl, and the heather was brown and dry. Arbitrary patches were burnt black where there had been flash fires.

Looking intently, she slowly turned full circle. No one there. She decided to move to higher ground and followed a sheep track that rambled crazily through the heather to a ridge high enough to cut off the view. From there, she was surprised to see a small coombe, green as an oasis, nesting in a purple-brown hollow below.

And picking its way gingerly uphill came a grey horse. Who on earth would come to a meeting on a horse, she thought, and focused the binoculars quickly. It turned out to be a fat pony ridden by a fat child. She let her breath go in a long sigh, and watched them. They were all there was to watch if you didn't count sheep and crows. Every now and then they disappeared behind hillocks or were hidden by a dip, but they always reappeared, plodding across the land-scape from left to right.

She glanced up as a heron flapped doggedly through the sky like an overworked coathanger. When she looked back the child and pony were gone She strained her glasses on the spot where she thought them likely to appear and sure enough after a short delay the pony galloped untidily into sight trailing its reins, saddle askew against its side. It came to a halt and then dropped its head and started to graze.

Anna heard nothing but the wind. She waited a few

seconds, and when the child did not appear she started to walk and then run down the hill. It was by no means easy. Heather tore at her ankles. She stumbled over rough ground and tussocks and jumped over small bilberry bushes. As she drew nearer, she heard above the wind and the dry rasp of her own breath the hopeless wailing of the child.

She saw her, sitting waist deep in heather at the edge of a blackened circle of burnt bushes, holding her arm tight against her stomach, hunched over and weeping.

Anna ran up, twisting a foot painfully as she came.

'Are you all right?' she gasped stupidly. 'Fall off, did you?'

The child raised her face, white against the gay yellow of her polo-neck sweater, eyes dark and shocked. She displayed her hurt arm. The arm seemed to have two wrists.

'Oh, lord,' Anna said. 'That looks nasty.' She sat down next to the little girl and put an arm round her, carefully so as not to jog her. She was about ten, plump and blonde. Her black velvet riding hat looked new and her jodhpur boots were shiny.

The wailing subsided into wet sniffles. Anna produced a handkerchief. The girl would not let go of her arm, so Anna had to hold the handkerchief while she blew into it.

'That's better,' Anna said, mopping up the tear-drenched face. 'Now then, tell me your name.'

'Sharon Goughman,' Sniff.

'And what happened?'

'It was that, over there.' She pointed with her chin. 'Pansy shied and the girth slipped.'

'That over there' was about twenty yards away and looked like a bundle of burnt rubbish.

'It's a skeleton.' Sharon started to shiver. 'It's horrible. It keeps smiling at you.'

Chapter 12

It was a pile of burnt rubbish. Definitely. Nothing else.

'Hold tight.' Anna slipped off her jacket and draped it over the child's shoulders. 'I'll have a look. There's nothing to worry about.'

There was nothing to worry about until Anna got within five paces. Then it began to take on human likeness. She circled round to the other side. The hair on her arms and the back of her neck rose in chill.

Something that had been someone lay on its side. No eyes, but a big, agonized grin. Cords of leathery flesh joined the jaw and cheekbones. The forehead was bare bone. There was some eyebrow remaining, some scalp and hair, but the ear had been gnawed almost back to the skull by thousands of tiny mouths. What looked like a nest of maggots stirred peacefully in a hole where the nose had been.

The charred coat flapped languidly in the wind. Beneath it Anna could see a red checked wool shirt. Hands emerged from the sleeves, one balled into a fist, the other, fingers curled like a lawn rake. Some of the end joints were missing. Thongs of dark brown flesh held the bones together.

The trouser legs looked empty, but the boots were in good condition; well cared for leather hardly touched by fire or corruption. How pointless, she thought when your boots have more life than you do.

She drew a deep breath; the first, it seemed, in a long while, and trudged back across the blackened space to Sharon. Her ankle ached. It looked like a long way back to the car.

She made a clumsy sling with the arms of her jacket tied round Sharon's neck, and encouraged her to stand.

'I can't,' Sharon whimpered. 'It hurts when I move.'

'Take it slowly and stop when you want to.' Anna helped her up. She wanted to get away as fast as possible, back to roads, the smell of petrol, people who smiled only when they were amused.

'What about Pansy?'

'Never mind Pansy. Someone can fetch her later.'

'I can't leave Pansy. My mum'll be furious.'

'No she won't. She'll understand.'

Tears started again, long panting sobs. 'She'll be furious . . . I'm not supposed to come out here on my own . . . If I lose Pansy she'll never let me have another pony.'

'All right,' Anna said in desperation. 'I'll catch her. But let's move on a bit.' They walked gingerly; Anna limping, Sharon taking tiny steps and hugging her broken arm.

They came across Pansy grazing unconcernedly and hidden from sight in a pocket of marsh grass. Sharon sat down and Anna walked over to her calling, 'Here, girl, come on.' She didn't know how to speak to horses and settled on the voice she usually used for dogs. Pansy turned her back and trotted away. Anna swore and followed. Pansy trotted faster.

Sharon called, 'She'll break her reins. She'll break her reins."

Anna went back to her. 'Have you got any sugar?' she asked.

'I'm not allowed to give her sugar because of her teeth.'

'Look,' Anna said slowly and clearly. 'We have to get you to hospital. We can't waste any more time.' Tears. 'All right. One more try, but that's all.'

She started off again, calling, 'Come here, good girl.' Pansy sneered, circled round and trotted away towards the body.

'Come here, you poxy, sodding cow,' Anna muttered, following. 'You stinking fat lump of dog meat. Come here or I'll boot you from Porlock to Minehead.'

They arrived back at the burnt patch with the horrible pile of singed clothes at the other side. Anna hissed, 'If you make me go near that again, I'll cut you into chunks and stuff you into a tin of catfood, you diseased, brainless tub of gut.'

The wind caught the burnt coat and it billowed as if the cadaver was turning over. Pansy skittered and turned to face Anna, ears flat and teeth bared. Anna leaped forward, tripped, but got a hand on the reins. Pansy ran backwards pulling Anna flat on her face on to the black heather. It scraped her cheek and tore her shirt but she didn't let go. She got to her feet and dragged the reluctant pony back to Sharon.

It took them over half an hour of painful, slow progress to get back to the car. By the time they got there, it had started to rain and Anna decided she hated horses. There was another problem too: what to do with Pansy. Anna wanted to tie her to the hawthorn and get to Porlock as quickly as possible. Sharon dug her heels in. Torn between the pain and shock of her broken arm and the hysterical need to look after her pony, she made a pathetic spectacle.

Anna couldn't bring herself to force a hurt and screaming child into the car. So she calmed her and settled her as comfortably as possible and waited as patiently as she could for the next passing traveller. It was ridiculous. The girl urgently needed treatment. Her parents should be informed. There was a body on the moor. The police should be told. And because of a bloody pony, none of it was being done.

The Goughmans, Anna discovered, were staying at the George in Quarmeford. The mother was a keen horsewoman. They usually rode together. The father had joined them for a long weekend. Sharon was not supposed to ride on the moors alone; her mother said it was too dangerous. Sharon had thought she would be back before her parents returned from a visit and that they would never find out. Now she'd be in trouble. She was afraid they'd take Pansy away from her. More tears.

The sound of a motor brought Anna out of the car. She flagged down a big red Rover. The driver rolled his window down. Anna said, 'Can you help? This little girl has a broken arm. I have to get her to hospital, but she won't leave her pony.'

'Ah,' began the driver unwillingly.

'Oh, the poor little thing,' his wife said. They got out of the car; the woman, all cashmere and tweed with beautifully ironed grey hair, said again, 'Poor little darling.' The soft heavy bosom worked wonders on Sharon.

'We're just on our way to Porlock ourselves, aren't we, Sammy?' the woman said, stroking Sharon's forehead. 'We'll take her to the hospital and stay till her parents arrive, won't we, Sammy?'

'Ah,' began Sammy with a longing glance at his golf bag.

'Well,' Anna said. 'I was going to take her to Porlock We just need someone to organize the horse and talk to her mother.'

'No, no. She'll be much more comfortable in our car.' The woman eyed the Renault with disfavor. 'We must help the best way we can, mustn't we, Sammy?'

'Ah, think nothing of it.' Sammy had caught a glimpse of Pansy who was still wearing her saddle under her belly and looking thoroughly disreputable. He was making the best of a bad job and Anna couldn't blame him at all. She cast a malevolent glance at Pansy and felt doomed.

The woman bustled around, transferring Sharon from Renault to Rover and tucking her in with a rug and a cushion.

'You will take Pansy home, won't you?' Sharon called anxiously. 'You won't leave her tied to the tree?'

'Of course she won't,' the woman crooned. 'We don't want you upset any more, do we? You will see to the pony?' she added more sharply to Anna, who was indeed wondering how she could best get out of it.

'Of course,' Anna said resignedly. 'And I'll find your parents. They'll come as soon as possible. Don't worry about a thing.'

'Good luck, old girl,' Sammy said sympathetically. 'You'd better take my card, by the way. Her parents might worry about perfect strangers driving away with their daughter.'

Anna also jotted down their registration number as they drove off. They were probably good people, she thought, but she wished they were the sort who preferred horses to children.

She unhitched Pansy and set off. It was roughly five miles

to Quarmeford by road, probably a lot less cross-country. But she had no intention of even trying.

Sometimes Pansy trod on her heels, dragging off her shoes and scraping her ankles. Sometimes she invented invisible terrors to balk at. Sometimes she flattened her ears and tried to nip lumps out of Anna's arm.

It was while she was tussling and swearing that a voice from behind said, 'Why don't you ride her? That's what she's for.'

'Pardon?' What Anna had actually heard was, 'Woi doanee roider? Thaz wha she'm vorr.'

A woman slid down the bank on to the road in front of Anna. She wore a voluminous fawn raincoat, probably from the last century, tied at the waist with a stout piece of string. A tangled mop of bright bronzey hair blew around her face giving Anna only the briefest sight of very pale blue eyes.

'Y'm be in a proper state,' she said shyly. 'Gave I a girt big laugh.' She giggled behind her hair. 'They words!' She took Pansy's saddle off and put it back in its proper place. Pansy stood as meek as a lamb, even rubbing her muzzle against the woman's sleeve. 'Tha's it, tha's it, my lovely,' the woman murmured, rubbing Pansy between the ears. 'Coush now.' Pansy closed her eyes in bliss.

'You can ride now,' the woman said.

'Not on your life,' Anna said, shaking her head firmly. 'Not a chance. Never could, never would. What me? You must be joking.'

'Ave t'walk then, woan'y?' The woman ducked her head and giggled again. 'This way.' She jumped up on Pansy's back and led the way up the bank and out on to the moor again. Anna followed, keeping well out of kicking range. But

Pansy behaved perfectly, showing no more temper than a pet poodle after a good dinner.

The woman was tall and very slim. Her feet dangled, out of the stirrups, below Pansy's stomach. But Pansy walked daintily, ears pricked, neck arched like a show pony. Anna glared balefully at her bouncing rump.

'Lil girl all right then?' the woman said over her shoulder. 'I'd'a come, only you were afore I.'

'I didn't see you,' Anna said, startled.

Another giggle. 'They never do.'

'What about the body back there. You saw that too?'

The woman didn't answer for a while. Then she said, 'Came for to take my pretty ones.' At least that was what Anna thought she said, but her back was turned and the wind was blowing. She tried to catch up and walk beside Pansy so that they could talk properly. But however fast she walked, the woman kept just ahead. They followed crazy paths up hill and down dale. She could never quite see where they were going or for that matter where they had come from.

At last one of the paths filtered into a broad track made by tractor tyres and they followed a dry stone wall. Out of it grew beech trees and grass that had been nibbled bowling green short by the sheep. The track eventually joined a road, and another dirt and shale track led between two high banks down into the valley.

'Down there.' The woman pointed. She slipped off the pony's back. 'There now.' She stroked her neck. 'Behave now.' She handed the reins to Anna and pointed again.

'Aren't you coming too?' Anna asked, thoroughly alarmed at being left in sole charge of Pansy again.

'She be orright now,' the woman said.

'Yes, and what about me?' But the woman had already

turned away, and was striding back to the moors, raincoat in full sail.

'Well, thank you for everything,' Anna called after her. But she didn't turn round or wave. She simply disappeared round a bend in the track and was gone.

'Bloody hell,' Anna muttered. 'Talk about the Spirit of Wuthering Heights.' She turned where she had been pointed, and within ten minutes was limping into Quarmeford.

Chapter 13

The George was comfortable: a white façade, a bright roomy lounge filled with bright roomy armchairs where guests gathered after meals to thumb through *Sporting Life* and drink coffee or brandy. It was after lunch now and Anna had to walk past several dozing guests to get to the reception desk. She was conscious of her dirty shoes and the mud splattered on her jeans. Above Reception a pair of antlers reminder her horribly of dead men's fingers.

On request, the young woman behind the desk paged the Goughmans and promised to ring the local police. Her eyes sparkled with anticipation. Something was up, and she couldn't wait to find out what it was.

Mrs Goughman was angular, jack-booted, and jodhpured. Her husband looked like new money, his coat a little too tweedy and his flannels too neatly pressed to match the splendid delapidation affected by old money. Anna explained quietly what had happened to Sharon and presented the Smiths' business card.

'Smith?' Mrs Goughman exclaimed loudly and very waspishly. 'You left her with strangers named Smith? What have you done with Pansy?'

'Where have they taken her?' Mr Goughman snapped.

'The hospital in Porlock,' Anna said, hoping he meant Sharon. 'The pony's in the car park.'

'The car park? said Mrs Goughman, as if she could hardly believe such stupidity.

'Shall I ring Porlock General, Mrs Goughman?' the receptionist asked, loving every minute. 'I can't raise Sergeant Williams.'

'Of course, ring them,' Mr Goughman said stridently. Everyone in the lounge was looking now. The manageress came in from the dining-room to find out what the raised voices were in aid of.

'Pansy could cut herself on one of the cars,' Mrs Goughman complained, making no attempt to do anything about it.

'Seven hundred quid's worth of horseflesh,' said Mr Goughman.

Anna was more worried about the Range Rover Pansy was tied to. She said, 'Any luck with the hospital?'

'We usually ask guests to scrape their muddy shoes before coming into the lounge,' the manageress said, just to add her twopenny worth.

'I have Porlock General on the line.'

'Here, give me that,' said Mr Goughman, 'I'll talk to them.'

'I really do think things could have been better organized,' Mrs Goughman said at the top of her voice to no one in particular.

''Things have been organized splendidly, Mrs Goughman,' said a new voice from behind the manageress. 'But perhaps you'd like to deal with your pony. It's threatening to damage the Colonel's Range Rover. Jenny, I'm sure the phone in the office is free. You could call the police from there. And Mrs. Norricks, I think the young lady might like a drink. She looks as if she needs one.'

'I'd rather have tea, please,' Anna said, hoping she wasn't looking a gift horse in the mouth. Although the last gift she wanted at present was a horse.

'Tea, Mrs Norricks,' the stranger said, 'and something to bathe that graze, if you would. Come and sit down. You look rather shaken.'

Suddenly the room was quiet and comfortable as it had been when she had first come in. Anna looked curiously at the stranger. He was younger than he sounded, but she couldn't put an age to him. His hair was quite grey, but his skin was tanned and tight except for the deep creases which cut from beside his nose to his mouth; a mobile, rather sad face with clear grey eyes which watched her sharply from beneath unfaded brown brows.

'Are you Army?' Anna asked, sitting down in one of the deep armchairs.

'No. I just hate fuss,' he said shortly. 'They love a drama, but nothing gets done.' He was wearing a black cord jacket with an open-necked, cream silk shirt and there was something beautiful, though a little too poised, about the way he sat. At once Anna felt uncomfortable about her own torn sweatshirt and muddy jeans.

The receptionist came over and said, 'The police'll be along shortly. They say would you wait here and they'll collect you.'

'OK,' Anna said. 'And what about the hospital?'

'Oh, apparently Sharon's out of X-ray and the doctors are

setting her arm now. Fancy that poor little girl finding a dead body like that . . .'' She caught the sharp grey glance and withdrew hastily.

They sat in silence till Mrs Norricks arrived with a tray. 'I didn't know whether you wanted any or not, Mr Olsen, so I brought two cups.' She set the tray down. 'There's hot water with disinfectant in it and some cotton wool. Shall I . . .'

'We'll manage. Thank you, Mrs Norricks.' Olsen dipped the cotton wool in the hot water and handed it to Anna. She dabbed the sore place on her jaw, washing off the dirt and dried blood while he watched critically.

'Milk and no sugar,' she said, to give him something else to do. He laughed suddenly and picked up the pot.

'I'm Ian Olsen by the way.' He began to pour.

'Anna Lee,' she replied, looking for somewhere to put the stained cotton wool. 'Are you the owner, then?'

'Good God no,' he said, startled. 'What gave you that idea?'

'Well, you know everyone, and everyone hops to attention.'

'Do they?' he said, smiling. Anna waited for him to go on, but he didn't. So she drank her tea quietly and kept her mouth shut too.

She wondered who had broken his nose. It had a slight bump at the bridge and a flatness lower down that she usually associated with profiles on Roman coins or old boxers. She thought she could rule out boxing, but with this sort of man one could never be quite sure. He seemed to be waiting for something too.

Sergeant Williams's arrival broke the tension. Subtly craned necks followed his progress through the lounge. Guests, unwilling to show impolite curiosity, were nevertheless aching to know what was going on.

He sat with Anna and Olsen and kept his voice down. He was accustomed to being the only point of interest in a well-ordered community.

Anna told him what had happened. He didn't seem at all surprised. 'It happens,' he said easily, as if it happened all the time. 'It isn't hard to get lost up there. Someone has an accident—the weather turns nasty—and Bob's your uncle. It's lucky you came across that little girl, because that's just how people get into trouble. She could've been there for days without anyone finding her. Young'uns shouldn't be allowed up there all alone. I've known folk lost only a few yards from the road or a farm, but as lost as lost can be.'

'It's a weird place,' Anna said, believing him completely. Olsen just smiled.

'If you've finished your tea now, we'll be making a move,' the Sergeant suggested, getting to his feet.

'Does she have to go there again?' Olsen said abruptly. 'It isn't very pleasant for her.'

'It's all right,' Anna said quickly. 'They'll never find it otherwise.'

'Do you want company?'

'No, thanks.' She hoped she didn't sound too rude. 'You've been very kind, but I just want to get this over with as little fuss as possible.' She also wanted a few private words with Sergeant Williams. And she felt on firmer ground with him than with Olsen.

Sergeant Williams drove a Land Rover. As they wound their way uphill out of Quarmeford, Anna asked, 'Have you checked your missing list?'

'I did do,' he said, looking amused. 'And I don't think it can be anyone local unless it's very recent.'

'Several months, I should think,' Anna said, feeling a little queasy at the memory. 'He was there before the fire.'

'That'd be end of summer or autumn, most like.'

They emerged from the valley on to the open moor. Anna pointed out the turning and after a while they came across Anna's car looking lonely and abandoned by the hawthorn. They pulled in behind it and got out. Sergeant Williams pulled on a pair of wellingtons and took a long white stake with a red flag on one end out of the back of the Land Rover.

'Which way?' he asked. Anna crossed the road and climbed the bank on the other side. The wind still raked across from the Severn, but otherwise everything seemed to have changed.

'We have to get to that ridge over there,' she said, pointing. 'And then you can see down into the coombe.' But when they reached the ridge, the coombe had disappeared. Mist lay in the low ground like milk in a bowl. There was not a speck of green to give her direction.

'This isn't going to be easy,' she said, embarrassed. 'The only thing I can be sure of is downhill. There was a funny woman here this morning. She'd be able to show you quicker than I can.'

'What woman?' he asked, and Anna described the Spirit of Wuthering Heights. He laughed, 'Oh, that's Daft Flora. No, we won't bother with her. She's touched.'

'Well then, I think it's this way.' She set off uncertainly. Touched or not. Flora definitely knew her way around, Anna thought, missing her footing, backtracking and starting again.

The mist hung like muslin and Anna was cold and damp when, quite by accident it seemed, they rounded a minor hill and saw the body.

They had come to it from the wrong direction and met it face on. Anna stopped and let Sergeant Williams go on alone.

He looked quite grim when he came back. He said, 'Did you touch anything, take anything?'

'No.'

'Only he's got this thing—bolt from a crossbow—I think, stuck in his side. Did you see that?'

'I didn't touch him or look too closely,' Anna said. 'I had to get back to the little girl.'

'All right,' he said thoughtfully. 'Well, the fletching's gone and there's not much showing, but that's what it is. I'd swear to it.'

He went to the highest point nearest to the body and drove his stake into the ground. Then they turned back uphill.

'He's not a local man, as far as you can tell?' Anna ventured after a while.

'How can anyone say, from that?' he said disgustedly. 'Got any ideas?' He stopped and looked at her. 'You're some sort of professional, aren't you?'

The unwelcome question. 'Yes,' she said. 'I'll give you a card when we get back to the car.' She hoped he knew the way back. Certainly she was confused by the mist and the dips and hollows.

'So?' he said, not moving.

'There's this chap from London,' she said slowly. 'His name is Edward Marshall. He was last seen in Somerset about seven months ago. He came down, supposedly, to buy antiques. But from what I can gather he also had some sort of sideline selling venison round the back doors of hotels.'

'Poaching Red Deer, you think?'

'I don't know. Around Frome it was roebuck. The police picked him up there. Can we go now?'

'What else?' he said, moving on.

'Well, I think he could be known to the Met, although they

say not,' Anna said, suddenly seeing the happenings in Kilburn in a new light. 'I don't really know anything about him, but he seems to be dodgy.'

'There's probably enough hand left to get a print,' Williams said. 'So you think it might be him?'

'Like you said, who can tell? I never saw him in the flesh. Just a photo.'

He walked on, slowly and steadily with the rhythm of a born countryman, but he covered a lot of ground. Soon they were out of the mist and into the wind. He said, 'Funny you being just on this stretch of road. It's the nearest point you can get to by car.'

'Yes. There was an anonymous phone call to my office. Some bloke wanted to meet me here. He gave directions to that lay-by next to the tree. But he never showed up.'

'I suppose I can check up on this?'

'You can call my gaffer in London.' To Anna's intense relief they found themselves back at the road.

Anna sorted out a business card from her bag while Williams radioed Porlock for men and equipment.

'Where you staying?' Williams asked, folding the card neatly into his notebook.

'Nowhere,' Anna said gloomily. 'I was hoping to start back for London since that geezer didn't turn up.'

'Mrs Meadows runs a nice B and B,' he said, giving her a straight look just to make sure she got the point. 'It's cheaper than the George and I know she's got room. Tell her I sent you. I'll call in later. Or maybe tomorrow if we don't get this sorted before nightfall.'

Chapter 14

Larkfall was a white-painted farmhouse protected by beech trees and beech hedges, and sitting inconclusively halfway down the hill between tame Quarmeford and untame moor.

Mrs Meadows showed Anna a room with a big, soft bed covered by a green candlewick bedspread and sporting pink brushed nylon sheets. A reproduction of 'The Night Watch' stood guard high over the pillow. She could have a bath in an hour, which was the time required by the immersion. Supper was extra.

What Anna really needed was the phone. She left her bag on the bed and went down to find it.

The house seemed to be all long corridors and tiny rooms. Either the walls were very thick, Anna thought, or there were more rooms than there were doors. The rooms were black-beamed and the doors had been built for midgets.

Mrs Meadows, rosy as a garden gnome in a yellow pinny, popped up from nowhere and showed her to the coinbox in a passage between the kitchen and the guests' living-room.

Anna dialed the operator and asked for reversed charge to London. She heard the operator ask Beryl if she would accept the charge. Typically, Beryl said it was too expensive and asked for Anna's number so that she could call back direct. Anna gave it and hung up. There followed a long pause, caused perhaps by other business, perhaps by spite.

She leaned against the wall, impatient for the invisible link between herself and the familiar world. With any luck she would catch Mr Brierly before he left for Waterloo.

The phone rang. Beryl said, 'Why do you always ring from call-boxes? Why can't you go somewhere with a proper phone?'

'You can say that now,' Anna said, 'but if I stay in decent places you have a fit when you see my expense sheet.'

'Compromise,' Beryl ordered. 'Now, what do you want? I'm nearly ready to close down for the night.'

'I have to talk to Mr B. And when that's over I want to hear the tape of that bloke giving directions.'

'I don't know if I've still got it,' Beryl said. 'And I'm not sure if the Commander wants any more calls tonight.'

'Don't try to gee me up,' Anna said wearily. 'I've had a bad day. Tell Mr B the local scuffers are on my back. And I know you don't wipe tapes till a case is as cold as your heart. So put me through.' There was a pause: a short one now that Brierly Security was paying for it.

Brierly said, 'What's the problem, Miss Lee?' Anna told him.

'Sometimes,' he said slowly, 'sometimes I wonder if you are not accident prone. It's a psychological affliction, you know.'

'There's nothing accidental about me finding that poor berk. That was meant to happen.'

'Probably,' he conceded. 'I gather you want to hear the tape.'

'I might recognize the voice.'

'Well, inform me if you do.'

'Yes. And I want to come home. I'm doing no good out here at all.'

'You stay where you are,' Brierly said sharply. 'If the authorities want you to stay put—stay put. I don't want to antagonize anyone.'

'But it's a waste of time . . .'

'Let me be the judge of that. Your time is well paid for. Refer any embarrassing questions to me.' Where, Anna reflected, the answers would have more to do with diplomacy than truth.

She listened carefully while Beryl played the tape. The instructions were exactly as Beryl had relayed them. She did not recognize the voice.

'What's the accent, Beryl?' she asked.

'How should I know?' Beryl said. 'I'm not a linguist.' There was a short silence. Then, 'Mr Schiller says Bristol.'

'Is Bernie there?' Anna said joyfully. 'Put him on.'

'All right,' Beryl said coldly. 'But keep it brief. We aren't made of money.'

Bernie said, 'Hello, love. Anyone you know, was it?'

'No. But it might've been a bloke I saw in Bath yesterday. And there's someone here showing an interest. I wanted to hear the voice, that's all.'

'Well, there's more reason than one. Who is he?'

'Ian Olsen.' She was now paranoid about almost everyone.

'I'll look him up. Are you all right?'

'Yes, but I want to come home. It's cold and I don't know the language.'

'I'll ring you after supper,' Bernie said sympathetically. 'Hold tight.' He rang off.

A light had gone on at the end of the passage. Anna went to investigate. It was a cosy room with too many overstuffed but battered chairs and a television. A man sat in the middle of the sofa knitting steadily, flanked by two loudly snoring West Highland terriers.

'Ah, company,' he said, looking up. 'Mrs Meadows said we had company. It's usually rather quiet at this time of year. Picks up with the hunting, I'm told.'

'Are you staying long?' Anna asked politely.

'Just the week, I'm afraid. My wife goes to Tenerife. But one can't take the girls, of course. Rabies, don't you know. So we come here. You don't smoke, do you?' he added anxiously.

'No.'

'I've just given up. It's so tedious, you know, thinking all the time about not smoking. Very negative. Never thought about cigarettes at all when I smoked. Can't think of anything else now. Hence the knitting. Something to do with the hands.'

The knitting looked excellent and Anna said so.

'So kind of you. Sit down, why don't you? Say hello to the girls.' But the girls seemed to be sleeping peacefully and Anna wanted a bath, so she backed out gracefully.

Supper was a taciturn affair presided over by Mr Meadows who was nearly as small as his wife. By contrast, the two sons were strapping and red-faced. They came to table in their stockinged feet, glanced at Anna, ducked their heads, and blushed. The meal was an odd one: home-cured ham and frozen peas, an apple pie from a packet with huge knobs of dairy-fresh clotted cream on it, sliced white bread spread with homemade butter.

Mrs Meadows said that Sergeant Williams was her sister's sister-in-law's third son, but as Anna didn't volunteer her business with him the conversation died. In a place where every family seemed either married or related to each other it was going to be hard work keeping her business to herself. But she wanted to try. Instead, she asked who Flora was. One of the sons let out a huge snort of laughter and the other one dug him in the ribs to shut him up.

'Don't you worry about they,' Mrs Meadows said, waving a spoon at her giant offspring. 'It's just Flora's a bit fifteen ounces to the pound.'

'Where does she live?' Anna inquired, wondering if she lived anywhere at all or roamed the moor night and day like a lost soul.

'That bit of pasture should be in my family,' Mr Meadows spoke for the first time. His fist hit the table, rattling cups and plates. ' 'Twas your grandfather Cox let her damned mother have the place. Bleddy fool.' He got up and left the table, his sons following. The Meadows men stuck together.

' 'Tis nothing but his silliness talking,' Mrs Meadows said, clicking her tongue in annoyance. ' 'Twould never have come to me anyhow. 'Tis only a scrubby old paddock with the old barn in't.' She started to clear the table and Anna got up to help her. 'But they do have long memories hereabouts,' she added, as if she came from somewhere far more sophisticated.

'Where is it, anyway?' Anna asked. The land, it seemed, was far more important than the transients who chose to live on it.

'Down by the river,' Mrs Meadows said. 'Scrape they leavings into the pig bucket over there. 'Tis about half a mile

Liza Cody

out of town. You can see the barn from the road. Proper
shack it must be b'now. But you won't see her lest she wants
you to. Right shy she be.'

'Yes,' Anna agreed. 'I don't think she'd've spoken to me
except I was having trouble with a horse at the time.'

'She's a rare sight with creatures, wild or tame. That I will
say. And she does do no harm to no one.' She plunged the
dishes into a bowl of hot water. ''Tis a shame to tease her.
But 'um do.' With this, she shooed Anna out of her kitchen.

The knitter was out taking his girls for an evening stroll, so
Anna watched television until Mrs Meadows called her to the
phone.

'Settled in?' Bernie said, exuding well-being from far
away. 'Cheer up, it won't be for long.'

'Oh, it's OK. But, Bernie, I've got this feeling that
everything's up the spout.'

'You've said that before,' Bernie said patiently. 'I'm not
saying you're wrong. But I don't know what's really worrying you.'

'Well, it's Mr Thurman, for a start. Who is he?'

'He's a client.'

'Yes, but should he be? I think we've made a big ricket
there. And then there's Marshall. He's got no family except
his wife. He's been missing for ages and yet no one's looking
for him except Mr Thurman. He's like a man with no shadow.
It's not normal. And another thing. I was told positively that
he had form. But CRO says he hasn't. Well, maybe he has,
only under another name. He's definitely more than just some
furniture dealer who owes someone money.'

'Look, love, we never get told everything. Never. Besides,
according to you, Marshall may well be right out of it now. In
which case, the game's all over.'

'Maybe.' Anna paused, feeling out of her depth. 'Bernie?'

'Yes?'

'You've got a lot of mates at Scotland Yard. Do you know anyone in C5?'

'Do me a favour,' Bernie protested.

'Those two, in Kilburn,' Anna rushed on. 'Those two heavies who warned me off. I think they must've been cops. So, one, they could be bent or, two, they might be C5. Minding Marshall. I know the old man says they're creditors like Mr Thurman. But they don't smell like creditors. They're protecting the Marshalls and they don't want me sticking my nose in.'

'Hold your horses,' Bernie interrupted. 'This business of the police minding grasses and handing out new identities left, right and centre—it's all exaggerated. Be realistic, love.'

'Yes. But it still happens.'

'What I'm saying,' he said heavily, 'is that it's very sensitive. Even if I did know someone in that department, they wouldn't tell me anything.'

'But do you?'

'I don't think they'd even tell me that.' A silence followed. Anna wished she hadn't started the conversation. She felt foolish. Bernie said, 'I might put out a couple of feelers, though. Because if you're even half way right, the further you go the worse it'll get.'

'That's what I thought.' She felt ridiculously relieved.

'Anyway,' he went on more lightly. 'This Ian Olsen of yours is clean. He's neither cop nor villain. If he's showing an interest, it must be your beautiful big eyes.'

'Ha-ha.'

'It's not unknown.' Bernie laughed. 'Besides, Syl says she

thinks she's heard the name somewhere. And if that's true he can only be Society or show business. Ouch!'

'Is that Syl leathering you with her rollmop? Give her my love.'

'She sends hers. And while you're on the spot, she's putting in a request for some clotted cream.'

'Done.'

Chapter 15

Anna woke up at five. The herd was being driven into the yard for milking. She woke up at seven. Someone was stealing eggs from violently protesting hens. At eight, she gave up and went down to breakfast.

Sergeant Williams was seated at the kitchen table murdering a bacon sandwich.

'Enjoy your lie-in?' he said, chewing mightily. 'I expect you were tired after yesterday.'

'Porridge or cornflakes?' asked Mrs Meadows. Anna declined. She also declined sausage, eggs, bacon, and tomato or any combination thereof.

'Breakfast,' Williams informed her, 'is the most important meal of the day. It's the only one you can rely on in my job. This is my second,' he added in a lower voice so as not to offend Mrs Meadows. She brought Anna a pot of tea and a pile of toast on the principle that what had been paid for should be provided whether the customer wanted it or not.

'This is not my finest hour,' Anna warned, pouring the tea.

'Oh, that's all right. We'll finish up here and talk outside. We don't want to get under Auntie May's feet.'

Mrs Meadows looked disappointed.

Williams's Land Rover was parked in the yard, tyres planted solidly in half an inch of slurry. He got in, saying, 'Let's go up the hill. You can breathe up there.'

Anna picked her way gingerly to the other side. 'You should invest in a pair of boots while you're here,' he told her kindly. Anna smiled, wondering what Beryl would say if a pair of wellingtons appeared suddenly on her expense sheet.

'I'm not joking,' he said, backing out of the yard at top speed, cow muck slapping the sides and chassis. 'You'll ruin them flimsy little things you're wearing.'

At the top of the hill, the sun burst out of its heavy winter clothing. The yellow flowers on the gorse beamed back. Anna was amazed. Exmoor was like a gentle rolling garden. But a few miles away to the north a man had lain dead, burned, pecked, eaten and inhabited for months without a soul noticing.

'What a weird place this is,' she protested. 'Weird!'

'It is that,' Williams agreed, as if accepting a compliment. He turned off the engine and pointed westwards with a forefinger pickled in nicotine. The hills five miles off were black under a huge purple cloud out of which lightning knifed and danced. He opened the window so that they could listen to the distant cracks of thunder. It was like living in two separate worlds at the same time.

'We don't often get people in your sort of business in these parts,' he said. 'Now, I made a couple of calls to that number you gave me, and all I got in return was one of them bleddy machines.'

'You should try after nine and before six,' Anna retorted.

'Londoners can be rather conservative about their working hours.'

'Maybe I will,' he said slowly. 'Only I wouldn't want you to think you could pull one over on me just because I don't work conservative hours. We aren't all turnip heads round here, you know.'

'Don't get paranoid,' Anna said, fearing a lecture on how whippet smart the local force could be. 'If anyone feels stupid and underinformed, it's me.'

'Well,' he went on, mollified, 'that's as may be. But I told them at Porlock what you told me and there's been a great big silence ever since.'

'Any report from Forensic yet?'

'Nothing official. Unofficially, though, it was a crossbow bolt. Poor bugger probably bled to death. And they've managed to get a couple of usable prints. But I doubt we'll hear more before Monday.'

If then, Anna thought.

'Now you say it was an anonymous call brought you here,' Williams continued, 'and what I really wanted to say was this: if you should hear anything more from the same source, I wouldn't want you buzzing off in that little blue car of yours without you tell me first.'

'You and my boss.' She sighed. 'The rock and the hard place.'

'I'll call him later. I've got another stop to make, but I'll drop you back at Auntie May's first.'

'That's all right,' Anna said. 'I'll walk. It might wake me up.'

'Watch them shoes,' he warned. 'And you'd better step lively, that weather's coming this way. You haven't even got a coat. This isn't Hyde Park, you know.'

Anna walked briskly between high banks topped by intricately woven beech, avoiding the puddles and the widely broadcast testimony to animal incontinence. Below, Larkfall snuggled deep in its protective hollow.

She arrived at the front door just as the rain began, and a black BMW nosed quietly into the drive.

'You look very meek this morning,' Olsen called. 'What are you doing out in the rain?'

'Inheriting the earth,' Anna shouted back. 'Come in. I'm getting wet.'

'Most of that inheritance is on your shoes,' Olsen remarked, offering her the jacket she had last seen supporting Sharon's broken arm. 'The Goughmans went home last night. I said I'd see you got your coat back.'

Mrs Meadows popped her head through the kitchen door, took one calculating look at Olsen's beautiful leather coat, and showed them into the front parlour. It was a cold room with a piano, herds of glass animals, and a log fire laid but unlit. An amputated stag's head hung over the fireplace on a polished wooden shield.

'Sergeant Williams told me where to find you.'

'Thanks,' Anna said, taking the coat and wondering what else Sergeant Williams had told him.

'You're staying on, then?'

'A couple of days, maybe,' Anna said vaguely. 'It's a lovely spot.'

He smiled, and they regarded each other in silence. It was a nice smile. Mrs Meadows looked round the door. 'Shall I make tea?' she asked, almost curtsying to Olsen.

'I won't stay,' he said. 'But another time I'd love some,' as if he was doing her a favour. She beamed. He turned back to Anna, saying, 'Will you have dinner with me tonight?'

'Um, well,' Anna said, caught off guard. 'I'm not equipped for anywhere smart.'

'The hotel, then. Seven-thirty. I'll pick you up.'

'No,' Anna said hastily. 'I'll see you there.' Experience had taught her never to depend on her date for the fare home. 'I might not be coming from here,' she added, so as not to sound too contrary.

Chapter 16

The post office in Quarmeford sold stationery, books and groceries as well as stamps. Anna thought carefully before choosing a large box of assorted milk chocolates. The picture on the box was of Welsh ponies with cute expressions hanging around on a mountain. It was topped by a glowing crimson ribbon.

She then drove out of the village, slowly following the twists and turns of the lane until she saw the old barn. The gate was tied to the gatepost with a jumble of wire and string which would take hours to unravel. Anna left the car and climbed over the gate.

The barn was a sorry sight with holes in the roof, only half a door hanging from one hinge, and one corner sagging. Next to it, on the lee side, stood a caravan propped up on bricks. The windows were glazed with cardboard, but it looked more habitable than the barn. Anna knocked and called softly but no one answered. So she sat on the threshold of the barn and waited with the chocolate box prominently displayed in front of her.

At first it seemed as if the field was deserted. But after a while it came to life. First, a one-legged jackdaw hopped round the corner of the barn and stood, head on one side, looking at her. Then came the cats, dozens of them. Once her eyes had become adjusted to them, she saw them everywhere: lying in the grass, under the caravan, on the roof. The place was crawling with them.

Two goats stepped cautiously out of the hedge and began to browse. And, further away, a half-grown pony moved out from behind a few stunted apple trees and peered shortsightedly at her. Anna wondered what else she had missed.

Time crawled by. She amused herself by playing with the kittens. The kittens indulged her until one of them went to sleep in her lap.

It began to rain and, one by one, the cats stirred themselves and went quickly into the barn so as not to miss too much sleep. Anna followed them, sitting where she could see through the broken door.

A few minutes later, Flora came striding across the field followed by one of the goats. She hesitated, and then came into the barn. Without looking at Anna, she collected a wooden crate and a bucket, sat down and started to milk the goat. At the sound of the milk rushing into the bucket, the cats sat up and took notice.

'Is that for me?' Flora said, peeping round the goat at the chocolate box.

'It's a present,' Anna said, 'to thank you for helping me yesterday.'

' 'Tweren't nothing,' Flora said gruffly. She got up, wiping her hands carefully, and picked up the box. She bent her head to look at the picture, her fingers tracing the outlines as if they were real ponies and she was stroking them. Reverently, she carried the box back to her side of the goat and placed it tenderly on the floor where she could see it while she continued milking.

Anna felt a lump in her throat. She wished she had brought something better.

'You've got eyes like my Daisy,' Flora said without looking up.

'Thank you,' Anna said politely. After all, Daisy had quite nice eyes for a goat.

The milking finished, Flora poured all the liquid she had patiently squeezed from Daisy's udders straight into a shallow trough for the cats. She didn't keep a drop for herself. Daisy ambled away. She didn't care who got her milk either.

'Can I open it?' Flora asked, hugging the chocolates to her thin chest.

'Oh yes,' Anna told her seriously. 'It's yours.' Flora unwrapped the cellophane without tearing it and put it in her pocket, neatly folded. She undid the ribbon and laid it smoothly across her knee. She picked a chocolate and sat sucking it solemnly, staring out at the rain with a shy, dreaming look. Her smile, when it came, was swift and elfin. She offered the box to Anna, who chose the smallest one.

'The ribbon?' Flora suggested tentatively, and pointed to her head. Anna obliged, tying the ribbon in her hair and fixing a big bow. It looked absurd, tawdry, and cheap. But, when Anna dug a compact mirror out of her bag and showed her the result, Flora was delighted.

'The man on the moor,' Anna said, after a while.

Flora nodded. 'They came in the twilight,' she said slowly. 'Like they do do.'

'How many?'

Flora held up her hand, fingers spread, thumb flat against her palm.

'Four?'

Flora shrugged.

'To hunt the deer?'

'But they'm gone.' Flora giggled. 'A long time. They'm been there,' she admitted, 'but they'm gone. There's many wants to find 'un. I know where they be. But I never tells.'

'How did they come?' Anna asked. 'By car?'

'A car and a van,' Flora said. 'You could hear they for miles. Silly beggars.'

'Was it a green van?'

Flora shrugged again. 'They did go down to Madacombe. Crashing about like machines,' she said, as if it were the worst insult she could think of.

'Were the cars facing this way, or towards the sea?'

'To here,' or rather, 'T'yerr,' but Anna was getting used to her speech now. Flora ate another chocolate slowly, making it last. She said, 'I thought: Cruel beggars, how would you feel, folk chasing you with bows and arrows? I thought: It's you wants shooting. I shouldn'ave, should I?'

'Why not? Thinking never hurt anyone.'

'No?' Flora obviously didn't agree. 'I ran away. I thought I did do it myself. Thinking.'

'Well, you didn't,' Anna told her. 'You wouldn't hurt a fly.'

'Wouldn't I?' Flora laughed suddenly. 'They flies is something terrible.'

Anna grinned. Flora was so pleased with her joke that she repeated it several times, laughing and slapping her thigh.

'Would you know them again, those men, if you saw them?' Anna asked. It was a mistake. Flora shied away immediately. 'I never would,' she said in a high voice. 'It were dark. No I di'n see they. No.'

'Never mind,' Anna said hurriedly. 'Don't worry, they won't come back.' She didn't believe her, though there wasn't much she could do about it. She changed the subject.

Flora told her how she had found the foal in the snow, half-starved, standing by its dead mother; how she had carried it home and reared it on goat's milk. She told of how the jackdaw had lost its leg, and a lot of other stories, some of which Anna couldn't follow. Like a lot of people who don't talk much, once started, she became overexcited and hard to understand.

In London, Anna thought, she might have been a bag woman, one of the pathetic band of London's lost. But here, she had her place, half way between the human and the animal worlds. A precarious place, to be sure, neither one thing nor the other, but she could live in it quite happily. Which was more than you could say for most bag women. There was nothing pathetic about Flora, Anna decided, when she finally left her.

She started in Porlock. There was no reason to suppose that Marshall had stayed there. It might just as well have been Minehead or Bristol or anywhere. She only knew that the van was facing away from Porlock. Then again, Porlock was small compared with Minehead and Anna didn't have all day left.

She did what she had been trained to do, canvassing hotel staff and landladies, showing her dog-eared snapshot, making herself pleasant to people who had no interest whatsoever.

At six-thirty she ran out of time, patience and energy. She hadn't finished. There were, it seemed, guest houses, B and

Bs and holiday lets in every lane for miles around. So she sighed and recrossed the moor to Larkfall in time to bath and change for dinner. Unfinished and unsuccessful; that made it an average day.

Chapter 17

There seemed to be a lot of electricity in the air that night. Dusk was illuminated by flickering blue flashes and thunder rolled around the rim of the valley. It did not rain.

They took a bottle of wine down to the river. A huge grandfather of an eel was reputed to live under the bridge. A lot of people had nearly caught it. But it was too dark to see. Instead, there was a tall plank of wood sunk in the river bank, painted white, and marked in yards and feet which told how high the water had risen in a long-ago flood.

Olsen said that up to a few years ago there had been a painted line, waist high, around the dining-room at The George to show where the water came to. There were even stories, he said, of a dead cow floating into the bar of The Black Horse. It had swollen so badly that no one could get it out again. The butcher had to come in and cut it up when the flood went down. Customers were given a pound of steak to take away after their pint. The farmer, whose cow it was, heard about it and sent a bill to the publican. But the publican refused to pay, saying that the cow was flotsam. The feud was still going strong, even though the flood had taken place some thirty years ago.

They walked back to The George. Moths were battering themselves to death on the illuminated hotel sign. The bats were having a field day, skimming in for a mouthful of moth and zigzagging away again at top speed.

Colonel Norricks was presiding over the bar when they got in. He was dressed more like a farmer than any real farmer could afford. He was just finishing a story, '. . . so he said to me, "I do like a woman who lisps," and I said, "I do like a woman who rolls her Rs." Rolls her Rs, comprenny?'

Mrs Norricks smiled sourly, and the men at the bar turned to look at Anna. She was the only woman present young enough to leer at.

Olsen said, 'Let's eat now, shall we?' and led the way through to the restaurant without returning the wineglasses and empty bottle.

'I used to come here with the family when I was young,' he said, handing her the menu. 'It was wonderful then. I thought it'd be ideal for a few days break now, but one should never go back.'

When the soup came he said, 'If you had limitless choice, what would you be eating now?'

'I see what you mean,' Anna said, looking at the fresh vegetable soup and wondering where the fresh vegetable was. 'Am I hot or cold?'

'First hot, then cold.'

'A ripe mango and, if I was cold, it'd be clam chowder.'

'Not bad. Mine would be a piperade, hot or cold.'

Over the braised lamb, he conjured up beef and black olives while she settled for chicken tikka.

'You're definitely Mediterranean,' Anna remarked when he fantasized a Tira Mi Sù in favour of the raspberry mousse they were eating.

'And you,' he said, pointing with his spoon, 'are completely indiscriminate. Soup in the States, entrée in India, and I don't even know where persimmons come from.'

'China,' Anna guessed apologetically. 'I'm the veteran of a thousand travel brochures.'

'All right,' he said, laughing. 'So, now describe the best meal you ever had. What I'm looking for is a theme.'

'An egg sandwich,' she said, laughing too. 'Sorry, but it can't be helped. It was when I'd just left school. I worked all summer, saved all the money I could lay hands on, and then set out with a couple of friends travelling round Europe, or the world, or wherever the wind blew. Only it didn't work out the way I'd imagined. I was fairly broke when we got to Turkey, and then I picked up some obscure fever. Well, Turkey is no place for a girl to be ill and broke. So I left my friends and went home. By the time I crawled into Dover, I hadn't slept or eaten for three days. I hitched a ride with two women who were going to London for the sales. One of them wore a blue hat with a bunch of cherries on it. I remember that because you never forget an angel. Anyway, she gave me a packet of egg sandwiches. And that was the best meal I ever had.'

'So it all depends on the circumstances,' he said. 'And if I were to ask you about music, for instance, you'd say it all depended on where you were and how you felt at the time?'

'That's right.'

'But the point of these games—' he smiled sweetly—'is to find out about the participants without having to ask a lot of boring, factual questions. In your case, I discover nothing.'

112

'The point of these games,' Anna returned, 'is not to show your hand. You've just broken the rules, and that tells me a lot about you.'

'What?'

'When you can't win, you disarm your opponent with a winsome admission of defeat and then swiftly change the game when they're not looking.'

'That,' he said seriously, 'is not at all a bad analysis. But it's taught me something about you too.'

'What?'

'When cornered, you attack.'

'So keep me away from corners,' Anna said lightly.

'I don't know if I want to, ' he said equally lightly.

Later, Anna dreamt of a flood. A body floated by, turning lazily, until one arm rose above the surface. The hand had fingers like the antlers of a stag. Olsen said, 'He isn't dead, he's only in love,' and she flew effortlessly up above the water and sailed away over green fields and under warm sunshine all the way to London.

It only became a nightmare when she found she could not land. Selwyn said, 'Stop messing around up there with your head in the clouds. Supper's on the table.' But try as she would, Anna could not get her feet on the ground. Just as she was about to touch earth an upcurrent took her soaring away again. 'Come back,' Selwyn shouted. 'The air's too rich for you.' it grew colder and colder. Anna woke up with all the blankets on the floor. A dog was barking.

Chapter 18

Mr Meadows was having elevenses when Anna came down for breakfast. It was 7.30 am.

'Late to bed, late to rise,' Mrs Meadows said disapprovingly. 'That friend of yours, Mr Shilling, rang up last night. I had to tell him you was out.' She poured the tea. Mr Meadows pushed back his chair mumbling something about dipping for foot rot and padded out.

'Am I to phone him back?' Anna said.

'He said he'd phone after breakfast. I told him when breakfast was, but he didn't believe me.' A smile creased her face. 'He's a very nice man.'

Half an hour later, Anna was talking to him herself. 'What are you doing, stopping out till all hours?' he asked.

'Having dinner with a friend,' Anna told him.

'Friends already!' Bernie said. 'Do you want some information about your friend, or have you pumped him dry?'

'Leave it out,' Anna said. 'I'm still half asleep.'

'Well, wake up. Syl thought you'd be interested. She had to

go all the way to the hairdresser's to find the magazine she thought she'd seen the article in. So pin your ears back.'

'I'm listening,' Anna grumbled. 'Just so long as you don't tell me he's involved in my case.'

'You still worrying about that? Well, he's not. He's in radio-phone communications. Some sort of cellular radio network. A big cheese, and something of a pirate, so they say. He took on British Telecom and beat them in their own backyard.'

'Really?' Anna said. 'How come?'

'Well, the government just gave him a licence to operate. BT fought it every step of the way and at one time it looked as if he was going to lose everything. They nearly fired him off his own board. But apparently he's very adept at boardroom shenanigans. He pulled some sort of sleight of hand and came up with every coconut on the shy. They say he's a dirty fighter, but then, you'd need to be against British Telecom. I just got the last quarterly bill so I should know.'

'Well, well,' Anna said slowly. She was pleased but she didn't know why she was. 'Thank Syl for the legwork, will you?'

'She's been more successful at it than I have,' Bernie went on. His voice was very thoughtful. 'I nosed around Victoria Street like you asked.'

'And?'

'And just about sweet F.A. But it's a funny sort of F.A. For instance, a request for identity came in yesterday from the Avon and Somerset force, complete with partial prints, possible name; Marshall. Normal channels and all that. Everything goes to the correct department. And then one of the nobs from upstairs, Assistant Commissioner level even, comes down and buries it. Since then, silence.'

'Silence?'

'I have a friend in records, and he had to field the follow-up query. He was told to tell Avon and Somerset they'd get on to it after the weekend. Sorry and all that. But he says there's nothing left to get into. The request and all pertaining documents have gone upstairs.'

'So what do you think?'

'So I think maybe Marshall is a bigger fish than we're supposed to know. And I think Mr B ought to be told. It's about time he used his connections in the old fart network. Only he's gone to Scotland for the weekend.'

'Damn,' Anna said. 'Did he find time to smooth out the local law for me?'

'Not half, love. You're a respected member of a respectable security firm. Paid up member of the Old Bill Old Girls Association. I bet you never knew what a respectable Old Girl you were.'

'Ha bloody ha. Well, that's something. At least I won't be clapped in the stocks on the village green.'

'Have they got a village green where you are?' Bernie asked curiously.

'Oh yes—the full rustic set-up. It's quite charming once you get used to it.'

'Even so,' Bernie said, 'I think it might be a good thing if you pulled stumps and got back to the smoke now. You being there might turn out embarrassing.'

'The old man told me to stay as long as the local law want.'

'Well, he'll change his mind, like as not, if it turns out you're right and C5 is on the other team.'

'And also,' Anna went on, 'I want to find out where Marshall was staying, and who was with him.'

'That's not your job now. Marshall's dead.'

'If Marshall's dead. If Marshall's even Marshall.'

'That's right,' Bernie said. 'It's iffy as hell. But if that body is Marshall, it's not your job. And if Marshall's someone else you'll get your wrist slapped for sticking your nose in. Either way it's a walloping to nothing. Besides, I thought you couldn't wait for someone to tell you to come back.'

'I couldn't, I mean, I can't,' Anna said hurriedly. 'But it'd be better coming from Mr B. He was quite adamant yesterday.'

'OK, love.' Bernie said, sounding as if he had a broad grin on. 'Only don't get too charmed on the village green.'

'I don't know what you're talking about,' Anna said indignantly. But he hung up without telling her.

Scattered showers, the weatherman said when Anna switched on the radio in the car. He was lying. There was a steady downpour all the way to Porlock.

She began where she had left off the previous afternoon. She began wet and ended even wetter.

'Good morning. I'm looking for a man called Edward Marshall.' Show dog-eared snapshot. 'He might have stayed here for a night or so at the end of September or the beginning of October last year. Would you check your register for me, please? No such name? And you don't remember the face? Well, thanks for your help, anyway.' And so on. Treat each one as if they were the first to be asked. If you behave bored or impatient, you get nothing in return except boredom or impatience. The friendly smile is what counts with most ordinary folk. Good manners and clean fingernails go a long way too. You're asking a stranger to take some trouble for a stranger. The least you can give is the friendly smile back.

By mid-morning she had run out of Porlock and was well into the outskirts of Minehead. She wondered if there were any corners to cut. Would Marshall stay at a posh hotel on the front, or a cheap B and B on the edge of town? Would he stay at the flash new place with the casino in the basement, or would he save his money at the quiet guest house half a mile from the sea with no view except of half a dozen identical guest houses in the same street? There was no way of knowing and no point in guessing. She had either to try all of them or none. And once started it would be nothing but a waste of time not to finish. It could add up to nothing more than aching legs, gallons of petrol wasted and a painful smile at the end of the day—and of course an encyclopaedic knowledge of places were Edward Marshall had not stayed. What was needed was a large team. One person couldn't go very far or very fast.

By four in the afternoon, she was as wet as she could get and the friendly smile was getting harder and harder to hitch in place. So she went back to Larkfall with no greater ambition than a hot bath and an even hotter cup of tea. Perversely, now that she had given up, it stopped raining and weak sunshine silvered the wet roads.

As she turned into the Larkfall lane she met the black BMW turning out. She pulled up alongside and wound the window down. Olsen said, 'I came to take you out to tea. Clotted cream and strawberry jam on hot scones. But you look as if a dry towel would suit you better. Where have you been?'

'Fishing,' Anna said, laughing. He looked wonderfully well cared for in his silk shirt and leather coat.

'What for? In this weather?' he asked, looking at her drenched hair and sodden jacket.

'A slippery fish. The one that got away.'

'Go and change,' he said. 'I'll wait for you here. If you

118

want to come, that is.' He smiled like someone who always got what he wanted.

'Can I drive?' Anna said, staring with admiration at his car.

'Aha!' he said triumphantly. 'She's impressed by fine machinery.'

'I don't know yet,' she said. 'Lots of sleek bodies turn out to be a disappointment.'

'Mine won't,' he said, laughing at her. She tilted her chin and let the clutch out. 'Don't be too long,' he called. 'I'm hungry.'

She changed into dry clothes and towelled her hair. Mrs Meadows said that no one had phoned and was she coming back for supper? Anna said she thought not. Another of Mrs Meadows's hybrid meals was more than she could face.

Olsen had left the driver's seat free. She climbed in and buckled down. They started off towards Quarmeford.

He said, 'I do like curly hair when it's allowed to dry naturally. It fluffs up like feathers. How do you like the car?'

'It feels a bit heavy.'

'What wouldn't, after that little tin can you run around in? You're smooth though, very smooth.'

Anna said, 'I was taught to drive by a man who made me take my shoes off and keep a raw egg on the dashboard. Nobody does anything sudden with an egg rolling about in front of them.'

He said, 'Take the Simonsbath road. You can let it go a little more there.' She took them over the bridge and up the hill on the other side, enjoying the quiet power of the motor.

When they came to the flat at the top of the ridge, they could see the huge sweep of moor and sky. The low sun glanced off hills and hollows, thrown back off new grass like light off water. The landscape seemed to be lit from inside. She pulled off the road at a place where the whole of the countryside seemed to spread out below them. The wind was gentle for once and smelled of something secret and antique, like an old sea chest.

After a while he said, 'Tea?' And she turned the car, and drove slowly back to a farmhouse just outside Quarmeford.

They had tea on a glassed-in porch that looked down over a sloping meadow to the river.

'Perfect,' Anna said, after the third scone. 'Just perfect.' He took her hand, palm up, and traced the fate line with his finger. She pulled her hand away.

'What's the matter?' he said, smiling, eyes half-closed.

'I don't know.' She sighed. 'One thing leads to another, I suppose.'

'Don't you like another?' he asked lazily. 'No, don't tell me—it all depends.' She said nothing, watching him narrowly. 'Well, what does it depend on? Timing? Pollen count? Or the winner of the Cheltenham Gold Cup?'

'Or is there someone else around who might get hurt?' Anna countered swiftly.

'No, there isn't,' he said slowly. 'I suppose I should ask you the same question. But I'm not as chivalrous as you appear to be. The answer wouldn't affect me in the least.'

'That's useful to know,' Anna said lightly.

'It's more than I know about you. Is there some sort of moral dilemma?'

'More an ethical doubt than a moral dilemma.' Anna

grinned at him. 'But not even that, if what you say is true.'

'What a strange woman you are. I can't work you out at all. You weren't fishing this morning either. Why did you say you were?'

'Metaphorical fishing,' she said. 'I can't help it if you can't tell fish from metaphor. And I can't help it if you prefer guessing games to boring factual questions. You clever people are always setting traps for yourselves.'

'And I suppose you don't. You aren't too keen on asking questions yourself.'

She thought that was pretty funny. 'Not to you perhaps,' she said, trying not to laugh. 'But I know a fair amount in spite of that.'

'Such as?' he said, looking intrigued.

'A cellular radio network,' she said, showing off and enjoying it. 'Car phones. You've got one in your motor.'

'Jesus,' he said, the corners of his mouth drooping. 'How do you know that? I haven't told anyone round here.'

'I read tea leaves.'

He passed her his cup and said, 'Go on then. Make a proper job of it.' She swilled the dregs around and dumped them out on a saucer. 'Well, well, well,' she said, peering judiciously into his cup. 'You like to be amused. You like concerts and theatre, but not opera and ballet. You like to be one step ahead of the crowd. You're always telling yourself you should read more. And you collect sculpture.'

'Cycladic,' he affirmed, staring at her. 'What a clever witch you are. All that from a teabag.'

'Modern seers,' she said, not holding the laughter back any more, 'don't need the actual leaves.'

'You're guessing,' he accused.

'Mmm. Have another scone?'

'No, thanks. Have you been to Doone Valley yet? There's a lovely inn that does a real old-fashioned steak and kidney. You can drive, if you like.'

'Okay,' Anna said cheerfully. 'My broomstick or yours?'

Chapter 19

On Monday, Anna went back to Minehead. It was still raining, but this time she bought herself a cheap umbrella and stayed dry. At about three in the afternoon she struck lucky. It was a small family hotel, AA recommended, with a false Georgian front in a narrow side street that led to the beach.

The woman at the reception desk was dark-haired and middle-aged but with a seaside complexion. A plastic card pinned to her blouse identified her as Mrs Susan Rose.

'There it is,' she said, pointing to an entry in the register, 'Mr and Mrs E. Marshall, second of October last year. I don't remember the face in the photo, though. He stayed for just the one night, and if I remember right, it was that glorious couple of weeks we had, so it was rather busier than normal for the time of year.'

Marshall had signed the book with an elaborate scrawl and had given an address in London which was not his own. There were eleven other entries for the same date.

'Apart from his wife,' Anna said carefully, 'can you re-member if he had any company with him?'

'As I say, I don't remember anything about him at all. It's my handwriting; so obviously he registered with me but that's all I can tell you.' Mrs Rose looked apologetic. 'Pip might know,' she added by way of consolation.

'Pip?'

'Pip Pearse. He's been our porter for the last year. I'll call him if you like.'

Pip Pearse was in his early twenties. He wore his oiled hair too long and his sideburns extended nearly to the corners of his jaw. He smiled a lot and looked as if he carried his brains in his biceps.

'I dunno,' he said, peering at the picture and trying to look thoughtful. 'It could of been him with the gun case, couldn't it, Mrs Rose?'

'I can't remember,' she said patiently. 'That's why we're asking you.'

'Yeah, well, it could of been him. He tipped me a fiver for carrying his bags and bringing him drinks. If it's him.'

'That would be worth remembering,' Mrs Rose said brightly.

'He had a gun case?' Anna asked.

'Yeah, only he carried that hisself. His wife had a lot of gear, though.'

'Can you describe his wife?'

'I dunno. She was short but big.' He made an undulating gesture with his hands and glanced anxiously at Mrs Rose. 'I think she had red hair and a lot of make-up. I can't really remember.'

'You're doing fine,' Anna said encouragingly. 'Did they have any company?'

'Yeah, could of.' Pip frowned. 'Yeah, that's right, couple

already here. They had drinks in the Marshalls' room. I went out for a bottle of vodka.' His brow cleared. 'That's right. They couldn't get a bottle from the bar. So I was sent out special. That's what the tip was for.'

'This other couple,' Anna said. 'Who were they? Did they come on the same day?'

'I dunno 'bout that.'

'What about when they checked out?'

'I don't remember,' Pip said. Then he smiled brilliantly and said, 'Wait a minute. His wife was crying. Don't you remember, Mrs Rose? You said how it was a good thing they paid in advance, him walking out on his wife like that in the middle of the night.'

'Vaguely,' Mrs Rose said, not looking as if any great memory had struck her. 'But so long as they paid, it wouldn't matter much to me. These little dramas are two a penny in the hotel business.'

'So you didn't see Mr Marshall again in the morning?' Anna asked Pip.

'Well, one of them wasn't there in the morning,' he said, losing confidence in his memory now that Mrs Rose had failed to support him. 'It could of been the other man, though. I'm not sure.'

'Did you see him go out that night?'

'No, sorry.'

'What about his car? Did you see what he was driving?'

'No, I can't remember anything else.'

'Well, anyway, that's wonderful,' Anna said. 'You've been a great help, Pip.' He went away looking pleased with himself.

Anna turned to Mrs Rose. 'Would it be all right if I copied

down the names and addresses of all the people who registered on the same day as Marshall did?'

'I suppose so,' Mrs Rose said doubtfully. 'I should ask the owner really. But he's away for the week. Just so long as you don't do anything that might hurt the hotel's reputation.'

'I won't,' Anna promised. She made a list of names and addresses. It probably wouldn't help. Marshall had given his name but the wrong address. There was no reason to suppose that his friends had done any better.

Outside in the car, she opened her A to Z and looked up the street in London where Marshall had claimed to live. It did not exist. Of the eleven other addresses on her list, six were in London, two were in Bristol, and the others were from Slough, Chippenham, and Manchester. Only three from London and one from Bristol had stayed for just the one night. Marshall's friend should be one of those four, if Pip's memory could be relied on. But a lot of mistakes could be made relying on other people's memories. And Anna knew she would have to trace everyone on the list. It looked like a job for Directory Enquiries, so she started back for Larkfall.

The police Land Rover was parked outside the farmhouse when she got there. Sergeant Williams was in the kitchen warming himself by the Aga and drinking tea. 'Hello,' he said. 'I thought you'd done a bunk on me. Auntie May says you haven't been home for three nights.'

'I didn't think you'd want me on a weekend,' Anna said. 'So I went to Doone Valley and Tarr Steps.'

'So I hear,' he said, smiling slyly. 'Pour yourself a cup and we'll go to the sitting-room for a chinwag.'

The sitting-room was cold. Anna sat down next to the night storage heater and held her mug in both hands.

'I've been hearing things about you,' Williams said, looking at her from under bushy grey brows.

'Oh yes?' Anna said stiffly.

'Your boss gives you a good report,' he said innocently. 'And my contact in London gives your firm a good report. So that's all right, isn't it?' Anna nodded. 'But it's reached my ears that a young lady of your description's been making all sorts of inquiries along the coast. Is that right?'

'Yes,' she said. 'Since you asked me to stick around, I didn't want to just sit here and twiddle my thumbs.'

'Well, you haven't been doing that from what I hear,' he said, grinning. 'At least, not your own thumbs. In fact, I've heard you're far from backward in coming forward in all sorts of ways.'

'Bloody goldfish bowl,' Anna muttered.

'It's as well to remember that if you want to keep your business to yourself,' he told her seriously. 'Well now, anything I ought to know?'

'I'm surprised you haven't heard already,' she said crossly. 'Or has the underground rumble let you down for once?'

'Now, now, don't take it like that,' he said. 'It's a small place. People notice things and they like to talk. You can't blame them. There's bugger all else for them to do. So what have you found out?'

'I've found out that Flora was on the moor the night that man died. She says there were three others with him, and they came from the north. And I've found out where the chap I'm looking for stayed on the night of October the second. What I still don't know is whether these things are connected or not. That's up to you, if you can identify the body. If you can't, I'll have to go on looking.'

'Yes,' Williams said, looking gloomy. 'Well, I'm trying.

That body doesn't match anything we've got on our local records. And London's being uncommon slow answering our questions.'

'All the same,' Anna said, 'is there anything you can tell me about him?'

'What? That might fit him with your chap?' Williams pondered. 'Well, there's no harm telling, I suppose. And it might save time if they're one and the same. Fair exchange, though. Right?'

'All right.'

'Well, as you saw, a lot of what he had on was damaged by fire. But he was dressed for hunting. He had no wallet, identification, or paper money on him. That could've been swiped, like his weapon. We think he must've been using a crossbow, probably like the one that killed him, because he had one of them heavy hide loading pads strapped round his waist. He had some spare bolt heads in his pocket as well. You could shave with them, they was that sharp. They was what's known as Broadheads. You wouldn't normally find them in this country. One of our forensic people said they'd come from Canada or the US. They're designed for big game.'

'Does that give you any ideas about the weapon?'

'Not really. The bolt that was in him had one of them stiff aluminium spines. The sort they use when you've got a really heavy draw-weight. The bugger of it is, see, we can't check. You don't need a licence for a bloody crossbow.'

'Don't you?' Anna was amazed.

'Bloody nasty things,' Williams agreed. 'You can buy them mail order, for all I know. It shouldn't be allowed. The bloody bigheads who buy them you wouldn't trust with a blunt knife and fork. Most of the good sporting shops won't touch 'em. And quite right too.'

'What sort of person would want one?' Anna asked.

'The sort as'd never be let near a proper weapon,' Williams said, wrinkling his nose in disgust. 'Them sort of macho cowboy types as live in towns. Proper hunting folk despise them.'

'The hotel porter I talked to said Marshall was carrying a gun case,' Anna said slowly. 'Would you carry a crossbow in a gun case?'

'I wouldn't've thought so,' he said thoughtfully. 'They have their own special cases as far as I know. Your porter mightn't've known the difference.'

'Probably not,' Anna agreed. She told him what else Pip Pearse had said.

'So that's it, is it?' Williams said, frowning. 'We have your Mr Marshall checking in at a Minehead hotel on October the second with a gun case and possibly not checking out again. And we have my chap, dead, possibly about the same time of year. The pathologist can't come much closer than that. And it's useless asking Flora what date it was when she don't even know what year she was born in.'

'Did your pathologist find anything else that might help?' Anna asked. 'Age? Description? Old scars?'

'Early thirties,' Williams told her. 'About five eleven and a half, dark brown hair, no eyes of course, well you saw that yourself. He said the liver could've been prettier so he probably drank a fair bit. But he was well built, heavy and not too much fat. There were two old fractures—one, very old, on the right wrist, probably from when he was a child—the other, more recent, maybe within the last five years, on the right ankle. Some dental work, NHS variety. He had gonorrhea. Otherwise quite healthy. They say the bolt went in left front. Pierced stomach and spleen. I can't say anything about visible scars, obviously. Well, there wasn't a lot of visible flesh around, was there?'

Anna dug out her picture and handed it to him. 'I was told he was about six foot,' she told him. 'Heavily built. Dark brown hair and medium brown eyes. There was a small V-shaped scar on his chin. You can just see it in the picture if you really look.'

Williams looked hard at the photo. 'Yes, well, who can say? My poor bugger didn't have much chin, did he? Still, I'd like to keep this. They can sometimes make a match by superimposing an X-ray of the skull over a photograph. I don't know if this is good enough, but we could try.'

'Can you copy it and give it back?' Anna asked. 'I still need it.'

'I'll get it back to you tomorrow,' he said. 'Anything else?'

'I made a list of all the guests who checked into the hotel the same day as Marshall. There was one couple there known to him.'

'Let's see.' Williams studied the paper she gave him. 'What's the stars for?'

'Those are the four couples who only stayed the one night.'

'Well, I'll have to go over there and talk to the hotel people myself, so you may as well keep your list. But you will let me know if you come up bingo on anything, won't you? Fair's fair.'

'Okay,' Anna said. 'Always supposing we're talking about the same bloke.'

'Well, I haven't got anything closer to bet on,' Williams said, getting up to go. 'You people can be quite helpful when you try. You work hard, anyway. When you work, that is.'

'Thanks a lot,' Anna said drily. He went to the door and opened it. 'I'd change my shoes, if I were you,' he said. 'It's bad for you, sitting round the house with wet feet. You should've taken my advice and got a pair of boots.'

'I'm not keeping you?' she inquired politely. 'I'm sure you've got enough on your plate without worrying yourself sick about my socks.'

'Oh, that reminds me,' he said, turning back. 'I'm not keeping you either. So long as you leave a forwarding address you can buzz off home whenever you want to. If you want to, that is.'

Chapter 20

It was time to call the office again. Beryl rang back immediately this time and said, 'I wish you'd stay in closer touch. I've been trying to get you all day. Your landlady says you were out all night. What have you been doing? You're not on holiday, you know.'

'A holiday's when you don't have to work weekends, I suppose,' Anna snapped. 'Or when I don't have to hear you preface every damn conversation with a minor rollicking.'

She was suddenly very fed up with Beryl and Brierly Security and anyone else who hadn't been out in the rain for five hours and didn't have wet feet. She thought she heard Beryl stifle a laugh, so she bit back the next bitter remark. Beryl enjoyed a scrap. It livened up her day and Anna didn't want to give her the satisfaction.

Instead she told her about finding Marshall's hotel and about the guest list. 'So I thought you might get on to Directory Enquiries and see which of those names and addresses are kosher,' she said at the end. 'They're all going to need checking up on.'

'Did you?' Beryl said sweetly. 'Well, let me tell you—I've got enough to do here without doing your dirty work for you too.'

'Oh, so sorry,' Anna said, equally sweetly. 'Well then, I'll just have to book into the nearest Holiday Inn, where there'll be a decent telephone in my room, and do it myself. You won't mind the extra expense, will you? Seeing as I'm saving you all that dirty work.'

'Give me the list,' Beryl said through clenched teeth, 'and don't think you're getting away with anything. The Commander wants to talk to you when I'm through.' She enjoyed a scrap, Anna reflected, only as long as she could win it. She heard the click as Beryl switched on the recorder. When she had finished, Beryl turned off the recorder and said, 'Is that all? Well, I'm sorry, but since you took so long, the Commander's had to take a call on another line. Stand by, please, and we'll call you back as soon as it's convenient.' She hung up without saying goodbye. You just can't win, Anna thought. She collected the mugs from the sitting-room and went along to the kitchen to put in a bid for another cup of tea.

While she was drinking it and chatting aimlessly with Mrs Meadows, the phone rang. She went back down the passage and lifted the receiver. 'Hello, sweetheart,' Ian Olsen said. 'I'm going to look at a cottage. Do you want to come?'

'Why not?' she said, instantly light-hearted again. Balls to Beryl. Two could play at that game. He told her how to get there. It was at the end of a mile-long track with a gate at the road end. He would wait by the gate to make sure she found the right turning.

It was about a mile and a half outside Quarmeford. The

road was wooded on either side with great beeches which met in a fan-vault overhead and filtered pale green light down on to the wet road.

Anna saw the BMX parked by a five-bar gate at the curve of the road. She indicated a right turn to warn the Cortina behind and slowed down.

At the same moment, the Cortina accelerated and came up alongside. Anna looked across in annoyance. The Cortina's window was wound down. There were two men in the car. The passenger was facing her, his arm drawn back to throw something.

She stood on the accelerator and the Renault staggered forward. After a faltering second, the Cortina caught up. She did not have enough power. She braked, spun the wheel left and hauled on the handbrake. The car seemed to stand still with the road sliding at top speed around it. The Cortina disappeared as she released the handbrake and fought to correct the skid. Then she hit the gas again and set off back towards Quarmeford.

In her mirror she saw the Cortina execute a perfect handbrake turn. The sort they teach you on the skidpan at police driving school. The driver wasted hardly a second compensating for his slide.

He was alongside her again in no time at all. She could see his yellow teeth grinning at her. His passenger was holding on for dear life. That was something.

She dragged wheel left again. But this time he was ready for her. He turned left too. Only a little. Just enough to dig the nose of the Cortina lightly into the right side of the Renault. Instead of spinning on its front wheels, the Renault lurched off the road.

She tried to wrestle the car back on to the tarmac, but it

thudded over the grass verge. She had a fleeting glimpse of the steep tree-studded bank down to the river. She stood on the brakes, at the same time releasing the seat-belt, and as the car toppled helplessly over the edge of the bank she hit the doorhandle and rolled out on to her shoulder.

She lay in a bed of wet beech leaves not moving, winded. The Renault hit a tree with a sick crunch, slewed sideways, and began to roll, tearing saplings and undergrowth in its path until it hit another tree and came to rest on its roof. The Cortina roared away.

There was a sudden silence. Then a blackbird sang. The damp earth smelled of mushrooms. Anna made a quick inventory of her limbs. They all seemed unbroken and in the right place. She sat up and began to brush the dead leaves from her sweater.

There were running footsteps on the road, and Olsen appeared at the top of the bank. He scrambled down to her level.

'Are you all right?' he asked calmly.

'Yes, thank you,' she answered politely. He stared at her. The lines beside his mouth were very deep. 'He drove you off the road,' he said icily. 'He tried to kill you.'

'Oh no,' she said. 'In my experience, killing is an accidental by-product of violence; not the purpose of it. Excuse me a minute.' She went behind a tree and threw up her lunch. When she felt better, she went down the hill to the car, switched off the engine and removed the keys. Her jacket and bag were hanging half out of the open door. She picked them up and went on down to the river. Olsen followed. She rinsed her mouth out and then drank water from her cupped hands. It was sweet and very cold. Her stomach stopped acting like a tumble-drier.

'Put your coat on,' Olsen said. 'Here, let me help you with the buttons.'

'They don't make buttonholes big enough for people who've just had their cars written off,' Anna said. 'Usually I wear something with a zip on these occasions. It's a lot easier and I can manage it myself.'

'This is marginally better than tears or hysteria,' Olsen said gently. 'But only just.'

'Fainting's best of all,' she told him. 'One loses all ability to speak. Very simple to deal with.'

'Why don't you just shut up for a moment? I want to get you out of the cold.' He took her arm and led her back up the hill.

'The problem with fainting,' Anna remarked, tripping over her feet and finding that her ankle did hurt after all, 'is that while it's beautifully ladylike and admirably silent, it's also extremely heavy.'

'Talk if you have to,' Olsen said. 'But also walk. I assume you can do both at the same time. I don't want to overtax you, but you are shaking like a pneumatic drill.'

When they got to the BMW, he switched on the motor and turned the heat up to maximum. He also produced a silver flask from the glove compartment.

'Drink this,' he said, pouting a shot into the cap. 'And try not to chew the silver off.'

The brandy burned her throat but made the rest of her feel better. She said, 'Did you see the licence plate?'

'No, it was covered with mud,' he said. 'Now I'm going to call the police, if you're feeling well enough.'

'I'm never well enough for that,' she said. 'And besides that was the police.'

'I suppose it's the shock,' he said, lifting the handset from his car phone. 'But you mustn't take this kidding too far.'

'Please don't.' Anna caught his wrist, arresting his hand in mid-air. 'I'm damn near sure that those two in the Cortina are on or were on the Met. I've seen them before, and on that occasion they offered to feed me my teeth in a teaspoon. There's nothing the local force could do anyway. They're long gone.'

'This needs a little explanation,' he said carefully, returning the handset to its cradle.

'Yes. And I suppose if we hadn't been playing blindman's buff with each other all weekend you wouldn't have to ask.' Abruptly, her shoulder started to throb and she felt drained and sleepy.

Chapter 21

Headlights swooped past, filling the BMW with sudden white flashes. Olsen was behind the wheel, his roman profile as impassive as a guardsman, watching the road. The wipers swung, rhythmically slashing rain off the windscreen as miles of motorway swept away under them like water under the hull of a powerboat.

'Glad to be going home?' Olsen said, after a while.

'Sort of,' Anna replied, stretching her legs and yawning. 'It's great for a holiday, that place, but it's very awkward working there.'

'I'd have gone days ago, if I hadn't met you,' Olsen said. 'I'm in transition, both in private life and business and I can't really afford the time off. It's lucky you were called back.'

'The early bath,' Anna said idly. 'Sent off for the late tackle and arguing with the ref.' Martin Brierly had been as deaf as a general at a peace rally. 'I want you in the office at ten o'clock tomorrow morning. I am trying to organize a conference with the client right now. You must curtail your activities forthwith. Hints have been dropped from high places.' Hints had been more than dropped from low places, Anna reminded him.

'I'm sorry about your car. Most unfortunate,' Brierly said stuffily. 'But it never would have happened had you waited to speak to me before rushing off. I know very well Miss Doyle asked you to. I would have told you then what I'm telling you now. The case is suspended until further notice. And that's final.'

Final it was. Anna spent a frantic couple of hours organizing a garage to winch her wrecked motor out of the woods, packing, paying Mrs Meadow, and as an afterthought, buying clotted cream for both Syl and Bea. Sergeant Williams had not been there when she called the police house on the hill, so she left a hastily written note. So many loose ends. None of the awkward questions answered. She did indeed feel she had been sent off with half the match left to play.

Olsen put a cassette into the player. It was 'In a Silent Way' by Miles Davis. Dreamy, lonely music filled the car. Anna knew she did not feel as disappointed or frustrated as she ought to.

'There is a great deal of renovation to be completed,' Olsen was saying. 'I should have been on hand to keep an eye on the builders. God knows what sort of mess I'll find when I get home.' He was talking about his new flat. All part of the transition he had mentioned.

'Stay at my place,'' Anna offered. 'Save the bad news till morning.'

'All right,' he said. Anna was surprised. Thinking about it, she realized that she had been preparing herself for the end of the affair as soon as they reached London, and her offer had been something of a feeler. They were not well matched in a lot of ways, she thought. He was too rich, too urbane, too much the high flyer; and while she did not feel exactly inferior, she knew they played in different leagues. And when they reached London, she thought, the difference would become fatally apparent. She had supposed that he knew this too, and if that was so, he should have tactfully avoided the circumstances that would make it obvious. But he did not. That gave the affair a new angle. She smiled to herself in the dark and said nothing. If he couldn't see her deficiencies yet, she wasn't going to point them out. Honesty was one thing, self-destruction another.

It was nearly midnight when they arrived home. Anna opened the front door quietly. But not quietly enough. Selwyn erupted from his flat, decidedly rosy about the nose, crying, 'Leo! Derusticated, by all that's holy. Have a jar. Let's celebrate.' He waved a beer mug half full of red wine, slopping a scarlet exclamation mark onto the wall. 'How was the "force that through the green fuse drives the flower"?'

'Forceful,' Anna said, trying to ease her suitcase into the hall, nearly driven back by the blast of words.

'Ah, the country, the thrusting buds,' Selwyn shouted, ignoring both her efforts and Olsen standing bemused in the doorway. ' "I know a bank whereon the wild thyme blows." '

'I know a bar where he a wild time has,' Anna said drily. 'It's great to see you, Selwyn. Now will you let us in?'

'I make all the jokes on the ground floor. Your platform's upstairs,' he roared. 'And keep your voice down, you'll wake Bea.'

'Sorry,' Anna whispered. 'Please dear, quiet Selwyn, let us through.'

'What's this? A souvenir from rural England?' Selwyn at

last caught sight of Olsen. 'Most holidaymakers are satisfied with a stick of rock.'

'How do you do?' Olsen said pleasantly. 'It's all right, I've got "A Present from Exmoor" tattooed on my chest. Will that do?'

Anna introduced them. Selwyn belatedly noticed the leather coat and the calfskin luggage which compared rather favourably with his Marks and Spencer pyjamas. He shook his head in confusion and the pencil lodged behind his ear flew out and broke its point on the ground. He stooped to pick it up and spilt more wine, stepped back and knocked over the bicycle. 'I was just off to bed,' he mumbled, backing through his door, leaving pencil, wine, and bicycle in disarray behind him.

'Is he always like that?' Olsen asked, as they climbed the stairs.

'Only when he's awake,' Anna said, opening the door. 'Unfortunately he's a bit of an insomniac.'

'An alcoholic?' Olsen said, looking around curiously.

'Just a poet.' The flat was chilly, but Bea had watered the plants and there wasn't too much dust. Anna lit the gas fire and opened a window. She leaned out. Nearly midnight, but traffic droned distantly on Holland Park Avenue, and the night smelled of rain and lime trees. It was very peaceful, she thought. Much more peaceful than the country where the call of owls and foxes shattered the deep silence of the night.

Chapter 22

The conference, such as it was, took place at noon. It should have started at ten, but Max Chivers had been unable to contact his client. He came alone at midday, full of apologies and more than a little worried. He sucked his pipe nervously and the two yellow-stained wings of white hair slid forward over his pink brow.

'In the end,' he said, speaking softly and hurriedly, 'I went to the Inn on the Park myself, only to discover that Mr Thurman had left an hour previously—somewhat precipitately, I'm told. He left no information as to where he might be contacted.'

'Unfortunate,' Mr Brierly said, snapping the lead in and out of his propelling pencil.

'To say the least,' Max Chivers agreed. They stared at each other across the bare width of Brierly's desk. Beryl sat, pencil poised over her empty pad waiting for something worth noting. Anna just sat. There was an unoccupied chair next to Max Chivers. He glanced at it and turned a shade pinker.

'Our two firms have had a long association,' he began. 'So I hope you don't think . . .'

'Please.' Mr Brierly raised a placatory hand. 'These things happen. No one is blaming you. However, it might be useful to know what you said last night to Mr Thurman that might or might not have caused his departure.'

'I told him,' Chivers said, sucking his pipe fervently but to no effect, 'that in view of certain developments, we should confer and perhaps take further instruction. Of course he wished to know the nature of the developments. I told him that the police had become interested in our inquiry, no doubt due to Miss Lee's discovery of a body on Exmoor. As you advised,' he went on, nodding to Brierly, 'I went no further than that. Mr Thurman then wanted to know if the body was Marshall. I told him that it had not yet been identified but that the police were pursuing the matter. He then said he would have to inform his principal.' He paused. 'You understand that this was the first intimation I had been given that Mr Thurman was not acting on his own behalf.'

'Of course,' Mr Brierly said politely.

'He then asked me to telephone him again in the morning, and he would make himself available for consultation.'

There was a momentary silence. Mr Brierly regarded the empty chair with equally empty eyes.

'Obviously,' Chivers said quietly, 'there may be a simple explanation for Mr Thurman's absence, but I think, equally obviously, we should take no further action until such time as he sees fit to, ah . . .'

'Quite so,' Mr Brierly said, looking as though he was thinking of something else. Chivers caught the look and sucked his pipe despondently. 'As regarding the fees,' he said at last. 'Although I feel my firm is in no way to blame, I think we can come to some arrangement.'

'Of course,' Mr Brierly said quickly and more cheerfully. 'No hurry. A more convenient moment will present itself, I'm sure.'

'My clerk will be in touch,' Mr Chivers said, rising to leave. 'Again, my apologies for wasting all your valuable time.' He nodded impersonally round the room. Beryl showed him out.

'Well?' Mr Brierly said, looking at Anna. 'I suppose you expected nothing less?'

'We could find him,' Anna suggested. 'If we started quickly. And I'd be very curious to see if Mrs Marshall has had any change of heart—if she knows her old man might be dead, that is.'

Mr Brierly sighed. 'Miss Lee,' he said, striving for patience. 'We cannot continue with a shelved case without a client and without the authorities' approval just to satisfy your curiosity.'

'Investigating Thurman might gain house points with the authorities, surely?'

'House points, as you put it, won't pay your wages,' Mr Brierly said, not without a small degree of understanding. 'No, we cannot continue, and that is that.' He reached into a drawer for a buff-coloured folder, which Anna saw with some alarm was her personnel file. 'Miss Doyle tells me that you have some leave due to you,' he went on. 'It would be convenient if you took it now. I was fully expecting that you would be occupied for another ten days at least, and consequently I've booked you for nothing else. Would that be suitable?'

'It's rather short notice,' Anna complained, considerably

relieved. Mr Brierly could be vengeful if any of his employees put him in bad odour with the police, whoever's fault it was.

'Admittedly,' Brierly said. 'But as you haven't had time off since—let's see now—yes, August last year, I'm sure you'll sort something out.'

'I suppose so, if you think it'll help with your scheduling,' Anna said grudgingly, but secretly delighted. It was a wonderful time to take leave, but she wanted Brierly to think she was doing him a favour.

'Perhaps you would use the rest of the day to put something on paper,' he suggested. 'Nothing too detailed, of course. Just to keep the books straight.'

Not only was she getting an unexpected holiday, but she did not have to write a full-scale report either. That made it an especially good day.

'I'm going out for a pizza,' Beryl called, as Anna passed her office. 'Do you want to come or shall I bring you something back?' Anna stopped in her tracks, mouth open. 'Er, you could bring me a Four Seasons,' she said, collecting herself hurriedly. 'I want to bag a typewriter while everyone's out at lunch.' Might as well make hay, she thought, going on to the Report Room. That morning, Olsen had dropped her outside the office. It was Anna's dubious good fortune that Beryl had witnessed the event. In a fit of ironic and extravagant chivalry, Olsen had jumped out of the car and opened Anna's door for her. He had also kissed her hand on parting. Beryl had come to a stunned halt in the middle of Kensington High Street, nearly losing her shopping-bag to a swerving commuter. It had done Anna's standing no end of good. But she found Beryl's bonhomie almost as revolting as her bossiness. Not that it would last long, but if she could get a pizza out of it, she wouldn't complain.

She began to write: date, client's name, purpose of inquiry, steps taken. After a while, she stopped and searched through her bag sorting out petrol receipts, mileage sheets, The Mendip Hills bill, Mrs Meadows's bill, receipts for meals. She clipped them all together and filled in an expense form. It was as well to take advantage of Beryl's unaccustomed approval. If she acted quickly, Beryl might cough up before the end of the day.

The phone rang. Beryl said, 'A Mr Olsen for you,' in her sugariest voice. Olsen said, 'Can you come over after work? We may have to picnic on the floor; the decorators have made the most god-awful mess of things.'

'Okay,' Anna said, hoping Beryl wasn't listening. Personal calls were discouraged and Beryl was a keen watchdog. 'Anything I can bring?'

'Just yourself,' Olsen said. 'I want advice. This place needs a fresh eye and a firm hand.'

'I'll pick them up on the way,' Anna said. He laughed and rang off. She began to write again, tracing Marshall's seven-month-old footsteps once more: London, Frome, Freezing Hill, Minehead, and finally perhaps Exmoor. There were as many gaps as there had been before.

Johnny came in around four and she put the kettle on for tea. 'Well, look at you,' he said, leaning his hips against the Rec room table. 'Blooming. Life with the carrot crunchers obviously suits.'

Bernie arrived when she was pouring out. 'Doesn't she look a picture, Bern?' Johnny said. 'Comes up lovely with a breath of country air. What're you doing tonight, young Anna? Give us a treat and come to the dogs at Harringay.'

'Give it a rest,' Anna said. 'Watching you drop your wallet on a crippled greyhound isn't my idea of a night out.'

'Nothing to do with a tall distinguished gent with a flashy motor, I wouldn't think,' Johnny said, blowing on his tea and winking at Bernie. 'Oh deary me, doesn't the girl blush? Warm your hands on it, Bern.'

'Beryl says you'll be off for a few weeks starting tomorrow,' Bernie said, and Anna told him about the outcome of the meeting with Chivers. She waited until Johnny had gone before giving him the pot of cream.

'This'll do my arteries a power of good,' Bernie said, well pleased. 'Funny how everything you like kills you in the end.'

Chapter 23

The living-room was filled with new reproduction furniture. The curtains were edged, draped, and flounced, and ruined the deep bay window. A carpet, the colour of ginger biscuits and looking as if it would have been better laid by a gang of Irish navvies, ate up the light.

'It's a disaster,' Olsen said. 'I should have found the time to do it myself, or at least I should have supervised it properly.'

In fact, it was a beautiful flat, tall, airy and with two bathrooms. Anyone with enough wit not to spoil it would have done very well. Instead Olsen had employed a firm of decorators who had probably cut their teeth on a banqueting room at the Hilton.

'It isn't even finished,' Olsen went on glumly. 'Nothing works in the kitchen and there isn't even a table to eat off. What am I going to do?'

'Simplify,' Anna said confidently. She was feeling full of bubbly assurance. Olsen's sad expression made her want to laugh. 'Fire the decorators. You could do it much better yourself.'

'How?'

'Look,' she said, hauling up the edge of the carpet. 'Look under here. There's a lovely old parquet floor. All it needs is sanding and polishing. And you could use white paint and get rid of all that dangling glass. The moulding on that ceiling's beautiful.'

'Can you do it?' Olsen said. 'I can get you all the help you need.'

Surprisingly, she found that she wanted to. She wanted to make the flat a place that was suited to him. And she knew she would enjoy doing something for him too.

That night, they wandered from room to room discussing what should be attempted, and in the morning he stayed long enough to sack the decorators and persuade the workmen to remove everything he did not want.

He was an extraordinary organizer, having no tolerance at all for small talk or excuses. He did not discuss. Having matters clear in his own mind, he just said what he wanted done. He wasn't heavy-handed either. He was simply convincing.

In the afternoon several men rang the doorbell and applied for the job of helping Anna. She picked an architectural student who knew all about wiring and materials, a young Australian who had very broad shoulders and a fruity sense of humour, and finally she chose a tiny Belgian drummer because he had holes in his shoes and had obviously tried to darn his cardigan himself. She never discovered where Olsen had found them, but they were all intelligent and tough-minded, except for the Australian who was tough and bloody-minded. Olsen said she couldn't have picked a more ill-assorted team, but after a couple of days, even he had to admit that they worked well together.

In the evenings Anna and Olsen ate out, went to the theatre or to a film. In keeping with what he affectionately referred to as her indiscriminate nature they ate in a different country every night: he knew Korean restaurants, Lebanese, Mexican, Malaysian, Israeli, as well as all the European ones.

Anna was possessed of a wonderful energy. She never felt tired and no problem seemed insoluble. She wondered briefly if this was the definition of happiness but quickly threw the subject from her mind. It was to be enjoyed, not thought about. Even the revelation of Olsen's wife was speedily dismissed. 'How come you had to buy all that junk?' she had asked him one night. 'Where are your own things?'

'My wife kept the house,' he told her. 'I should have told you before, but you seemed to know everything else. We split up a few months ago. It was during the time I was having so much trouble. My partner went for a hundred per cent take over; Tel-Cel, Olivia, the lot. Olivia went to him when it looked as if he was succeeding. She has a huge appetite for power. I won back Tel-Cel, as you know.'

'And your partner?'

'Is no longer my partner,' he said coldly. His eyes behind half-lowered lids, glittered with something quite ruthless. Anna changed the subject.

At times when Olsen's flat was too full of sawdust or the smell of paint, they went to Anna's. Bea adored him. Selwyn was impressed but had doubts. 'he's too bloody forceful by half,' he said moodily, on one of the rare occasions they were together without Olsen. 'You mark my words. You're no match for him, Leo. He's already got you dancing to his tune.'

'Now there's a proper man,' Bea said dreamily. She had taken to putting up her hair and wearing her best frocks when Olsen came.

'Who's a proper man?' Selwyn cried, incensed. 'You're talking to a man who's about to be published. At someone else's expense this time.' This was a small collection of Selwyn's work called *Blues in the Red*. His admiration for himself at this time was boundless and he could not bear to be upstaged. 'It's bloody famous I'll be,' he informed them, and the neighbours too, if they'd been listening. 'Among the cognoscenti, anyway,' he amended more quietly and certainly more accurately, 'I'm a proper man of letters, and it's bloody silly you'll look making sheep's eyes at a mere industrial warlord.'

'Captain of industry, you mean,' Bea said huffily.

'I know what I mean,' Selwyn shouted. 'And I know a warlord when I see one. You want to watch out, Leo, or you'll become a prisoner of war. Look at Bea. She's a slave-state all by herself.' He ducked quickly but Bea, aiming low, caught him full in the face with a cushion.

At his insistence, Olsen's study was the first room to be completed. And when Anna could promise there would be no more dust or power tools, he brought a group of his own people to install the equipment. The result was a pleasing combination of library and high-tech office. A computer linked him with both his works and head office. And of course there were the phones: the ones he was developing himself as well as the ordinary ones. Olsen liked to be in touch wherever he chose to be. Activity followed him everywhere, and whenever he came home at odd times during the day, phones rang, messengers came and the telex chattered.

David, the architectural student, began to refer to him as Ground Control. The name caught on.

The weather improved, and it was bright and sunny on the day they finished the drawing-room.

'I say, it's turned out rather well,' David said, when they took a last admiring look at it before moving on to other tasks.

'Too bloody right it has,' Barry muttered.

'*Magnifique!*' said Hervé. It had turned out much as Anna had hoped it would; a classical Georgian shape with a deeply shining floor.

'No curtains,' David said. 'Just blinds. We mustn't spoil that bay.'

'A piano,' suggested Hervé, and they all silently imagined an open Steinway by the window.

'Can Ground Control play the poxy piano?' Barry asked, bringing them all back to earth. Anna had to admit that she didn't know.

If she stopped to think about it, she would have had to admit that there was a lot she did not know about Olsen. Did he, for instance, have a family? If he had, she had not met any members of it. Nor had she met anyone who claimed to be a close friend. Olsen had such an air of completeness about him it was as if he had popped, utterly self-sufficient, into the world; as he had into her life—in every way a self-made man.

If she had been asked, she would have said that she was too busy to ask herself questions. The days were too hectic and the nights too joyous. She was trained to ask questions, and it was one of her firm beliefs that acting blindly, when there was sufficient information to be had for the asking, was foolish and in the end self-defeating. Professionally, she understood that to stop asking questions when she had enough information to satisfy herself was also dangerous.

But like so many professional people, she did not apply professional standards to private matters. In fact, she lived entirely in the present. She no longer dreamed of the half-decayed, half-burnt body on Exmoor, or wondered who Marshall was. The questions about Mr Thurman's disappearance and whether or not Yellow Fang was a policeman did not concern her. Nor could she imagine going back to the office or any other future problem.

Chapter 24

When the major alterations were complete, Anna turned Barry and Hervé out into the garden. Neither they nor she knew a lot about gardening, but it was in such a mess that initially all that was needed was enthusiasm. David addressed himself to the rest of the interior decoration, searching London for Turkish rugs and chesterfields and all the other things they needed to finish the job.

Anna found herself alone in the big flat for longer periods of time. It was, without doubt, a very pleasant place to be.

Late on one such morning, the doorbell rang. Anna went to answer it, and found a woman on the doorstep. She knew without being told that this was Olivia Olsen.

With a sudden jolt of awareness, she knew too that if she had been asked to choose a woman for Olsen, as she had been asked to choose a dining-room table, she would have chosen Olivia. She was tall with smooth dark hair and a lustrous skin. When she walked into the hall Anna saw in an instant that, from her jersey silk dress to her soft kid boots, she suited the flat that Anna had designed to suit Olsen. It was a shocking moment.

'Is Yan here?' she asked in a voice that was soft and a little husky.

'No,' Anna mumbled, busily wiping varnish off her fingers. 'And I don't know when he'll be back.'

'Of course not,' Olivia said in a friendly way. 'No one ever does.'

'I'll give him a message, if you like,' Anna said, hoping Olivia would leave immediately.

'No need,' Olivia said, looking at Anna with amused, intelligent eyes. They were almost the same colour as Olsen's. 'You must be Yan's new friend,' she went on. 'Well, you've certainly made a wonderful job of the flat. I have to admit, it's really rather special.'

'Thanks,' Anna said, still mumbling and rubbing nervously at her hands.

'You don't happen to have a drink in the house, do you?' Olivia asked. 'Oh, of course you do. White wine in the fridge.' Anna dumbly led the way to the kitchen and fetched wine from the fridge, and a glass and corkscrew from the cupboard.

'How nice, Sancerre, my favourite,' Olivia said, opening the bottle with a graceful twist of her wrist. 'Will you join me? We really ought to talk, you know.'

'I'll make tea,' Anna said, turning her back to fill the kettle and escape the sight of Olivia in Olsen's new kitchen. If she had been an ostrich, she would have buried her head.

'I imagine there's a nice piece of Caerphilly in the fridge too,' Olivia said, smiling pleasantly.

'Help yourself.'

'I'm afraid, you know, that I've come to give you notice,'

Olivia said, with what sounded like genuine regret. She cut a slice of cheese cleanly and efficiently as if demonstrating what she meant to do to Anna.

'Oh yes?' Anna said. 'I don't think that's quite up to you.'

'I think you'll find that it is.' She quartered an apple and offered it to Anna. 'Will you mind frightfully? I'm so very sorry.' She looked as though she meant it. 'Look, I want to be absolutely straightforward about this. I am three and a half months pregnant.'

'Congratulations,' Anna said stupidly.

'Thank you. If it weren't for that, I could have allowed this affair to run its course.'

'Run its course?' Anna asked. She moved so that her back was to the light. She didn't want Olivia to see the expression on her face.

'I'm thinking of you, actually,' Olivia said, leaning her cheek against her knuckles and regarding Anna with clear grey eyes that held a lot of sympathy. 'You are a very independent woman, I'm told. So when the flat is finished, what will you do then? What will you be able to contribute, I mean?' Olivia had so surely uncovered a deeply buried anxiety that Anna was left speechless. 'I think you would feel, well, impotent, if you see what I mean.' With awful clarity, Anna saw exactly what she meant. 'Forgive me for saying so,' Olivia went on, 'but without denying the qualities you undoubtedly do possess, I can't see you being happy without a real gift to give.'

'Please don't patronize me,' Anna said with difficulty, but finding her tongue at last. 'Everything you say may or may not be true, but it's absolutely no business of yours. If you want to talk to me, let's talk about your problems. Because it seems to me that, in spite of your concern for my welfare, what you're doing is trying to choose a father for your child.'

'Well put,' Olivia said calmly. 'But what if I told you that Ian is, without any doubt, the father?'

'If that was true you'd have already said so.'

'Quite,' Olivia said, unruffled.

'And Olsen? Does he know about this?'

'Of course he knows.'

'And how does he feel about being elected father?'

Olivia smiled. 'He hasn't said. But if I know him at all, he won't want anyone else to bring up his child. You will say, rightly, that it may not be his child. But I think he'll take that chance.'

'This other man. Why're you giving him the chop now? You chose him.'

'That was a mistake,' Olivia said. 'He never really had what it takes, so to speak. But it's a mistake I can rectify.'

'Can you?' Anna asked grimly.

'Oh yes. I'm sorry, but I think I can.'

'Don't apologize,' Anna said. 'Just sling your hook.'

'Very well.' Olivia got up and went to the door. 'I do understand how you feel.'

'No, you don't,' Anna said positively. 'Or you wouldn't turn your back.'

Chapter 25

What do I do now? Anna thought, slamming the door furiously, get pregnant myself just to be competitive? There was no sound from the Prices' flat. Selwyn would still be at the pub.

Olivia was just the type, she thought, to have two men queueing up to be the father of her child, when most women in similar circumstances found it difficult to persuade even one. She found an old Blood Sweat and Tears album and put it on the hi-fi. She was concentrating her feelings on Olivia's pregnancy because she did not want to face the other aspects of their conversation. She turned the volume up very loud. The phone rang.

When the pips stopped, a woman's voice said, 'I kept your card. You said to ring if I wanted to talk.'

'It took Anna a couple of seconds to place the voice. 'Jane Marshall?' she asked.

'I'm in a call-box and I haven't much silver. Did you find Edward?'

'I though you didn't want me to look.'

'That was then,' Jane said quickly. 'I changed my mind. Can we meet somewhere?'

'I don't know,' Anna said. She did not want to go out in case Olsen phoned. 'I'm not on the job any more. My boss'd go spare.'

'You said if I wanted any help,' Jane persisted. 'And I got trouble now.'

'All right.' Anna changed her mind suddenly. Anyone else's troubles were more attractive than her own. 'Where?'

'I dunno. You know there's people keeping an eye on me?'

'Yeah. Are they around now?'

'I dunno. I think so. They said not to talk to you. I'm scared of them.'

'I tell you what,' Anna said, thinking quickly. 'Go to Selfridge's. Can you get there in half an hour?'

'Then what?'

'The Miss Selfridge department. Know it? Well, pick yourself a couple of dresses and go into the fitting rooms. I'll meet you there.'

'That's good.' Jane Marshall giggled. 'See you.' She rang off. Anna grabbed her coat and bag and left the flat.

She got off the bus outside Selfridge's and dodged through the crowds of shoppers, Hari Krishnas, and bunking-off schoolgirls into Duke Street. The plate glass windows gave a good view into the shop. Anna peered past the dummies. There were only women inside. She went in. She snatched a couple of skirts indiscriminately from the racks and made her way into the changing room. It was not empty. Several women in varying stages of undress struggled with hangers and zips, all rather uncomfortable about showing their underwear in public.

'I quite fancy the red one,' Jane Marshall said, coming in behind Anna. 'Might as well try it on while I'm here.'

Anna sat on a stool and held Jane's bag as she stripped off shirt and skirt. She was wearing a lime green bra and slip underneath, and Anna watched fascinated as she wriggled into the brilliant scarlet creation she had brought with her.

'Is Edward dead?' she asked matter of factly as her flushed face appeared out of the neck hole.

'I honestly don't know,' Anna said.

'I'm really sorry I couldn't tell you nothing when you came before. But what with them around and I swore I'd never. I still can't, really. Zip me up, will you?' Anna zipped her up. 'You know they're filth, don't you?' Jane went on, smoothing the red ruffles on her chest. 'I'm not even supposed to say that, but I just got to talk to someone. I just got to know.' She turned sideways to the mirror and examined her profile. 'Makes me look top-heavy, dunnit?'

'It's the ruffles,' Anna said tactfully.

'Pity. Red's me favourite colour. Still, the blue's not bad neither. Might as well try that too.'

Anna unzipped the red. 'Tell me something about Edward,' she suggested.

'Such as?' Jane said, worming her way out of the red and into the blue. 'I can't say much. Really I can't.' She seemed to favour clothes that fitted her snugly.

'Such as, when did he break his right ankle?' Anna asked awkwardly. She could not think of a kind way to do it.

''How'd you know that?' Jane said, perplexed. 'Zip?' Anna zipped. 'He fell over the dog one night when he'd had a few'

'I didn't know you had a dog.'

'We haven't now.' Jane tightened the belt and undid a button at the chest. 'Not after that. The dog bit him. Startled, see? And Edward fell down the stairs trying to get away. What do you think?' She spun round.

'Better,' Anna said. 'It's nice with your colouring.'

'I've got too much blue already. I always end up with blue.' Anna unzipped the blue. 'He said his right was his unlucky side,' Jane said, emerging from the dress and handing it to Anna to hang up before diving head first into something yellow and white.

Anna took a deep breath, and asked, 'Because of his wrist, when he was a kid?' She felt awful about it.

'Yeah. You did find him, didn't you?' Jane stood upright, tousled and all undone.

'I think I must have done,' Anna said sadly. 'I'm sorry.'

'He's dead, isn't he? Go on, you can tell me,' Jane said in a small voice. 'I'd rather know.'

'Sit down, love,' Anna said, making room for her. 'I was hoping it wasn't him. But now I think it must be.' Jane sat with her plump legs stuck straight out in front of her. She seemed to be staring at her own knees. Anna couldn't see her face.

'Do you want to go somewhere else?' Anna asked. 'This was a rotten place to tell you.'

'No. I like it,' Jane said, lifting her head. Her eyes were a little pink, but that was all. 'I won't let meself down here. I'm not shocked or anything. He's been away so long. I just knew something had happened to him. I knew it. And them two gits've been acting really queer lately.' They sat quietly for a while. Then Jane said, 'I suppose I ought to get something black while I'm here.' She sniffed and giggled miserably. 'It's not like he was a wonderful husband or anything. It's just, well, you know.'

'I know.'

'I'm glad you told me. Really.' She straightened up. 'What happened?' Anna told her as much as she could without going into details. Then she said, 'There were two others with him. I think one of them at least came from the West Country—Bristol perhaps. Does that ring a bell?'

'Greg bleeding Morland,' Jane said, flushing angrily. 'I'll bleeding swing for him, I will! They was in the Paras together. He's been a pain in the arse ever since I known him. He organized Edward's stag night for him. Big favour. Edward was still paralytic at the church next morning. They had blue movies and girls and every disgusting thing you can think of. I know 'cos my very good friend Cindy told me all about it. I think that's filthy, just before your wedding, don't you?'

'I can't understand men at all sometimes,' Anna said, agreeing.

'Nor me neither.' Jane sighed. 'I can't, really. I mean, have a few drinks and a bit of fun, yes. But all that dirty stuff just before your wedding. That's Greg Morland all over—a spoiler—always going too far. It's funny, really. He says he loves women, can't keep away from them. But he doesn't. I think he hates us. That's why he's always knocking marriage. And he always wants his mates to do the same. Always getting the boys together doing something us girls aren't supposed to know about. Big deal. And that poaching stunt. That'd be just his scene. Get all the boys out of a night doing something hairy.'

'Did Edward have a crossbow?'

'Not in my house, he didn't,' Jane said harshly. 'But what would I know? They was always on about weapons. You know, reading all the gun magazines and that. Man's talk.' She snorted sarcastically. 'Never recovered from the bleeding army, if you ask me.'

'This buying trip to the West Country—did he go often?'

Jane thought about it, twisting her wedding ring round and round. She said, 'Once or twice. There's a lot of house sales and auctions round there, he said. But I ask myself now, why not Wales or Yorkshire? If he was seeing bleeding Greg, he would've kept mum to me. He knew how I felt about the bleeder.' With an abrupt twist of her hands the wedding ring came loose and flew out of her fingers. It rolled across the fitting room floor and came to rest by another woman's feet. Jane got up and retrieved it. She said, 'What's so tragic is this was supposed to be a fresh start. And he blows it all away 'cos he can't keep clear of the dodgy stuff.'

'Fresh start from what?'

Jane stared at her, still standing. 'I never can tell you that,' she said. 'So don't ask me. It's not I don't trust you. It's just I swore I'd never. Shall I look for something black?'

'You might as well,' Anna said, thinking it might make her feel better if she did. 'And while you're out there, have a look in case someone's waiting for you.' She sat alone for a while, thinking about women in communal changing rooms. She doubted if Jane would have told her so much anywhere else. As if all the dressing and undressing led to a false sense of trust and intimacy. Then she thought about herself and Olsen and wondered if that intimacy really existed either.

Jane came back with two black numbers and started to strip again. She said, 'No one out there,' and disappeared into the depths of the first dress. When she emerged she went on, 'And another thing: it's money, really. That's why I rang, really. I'm very short of cash now. The stock's all run down and I didn't know what to do. Zip?' Anna zipped. 'I'll sell out now, I suppose. What do you think?'

'You could do, if you don't want to carry on on your own.'

'The dress, silly,' Jane said, turning round, 'No, I'll be all right about the shop, so long as I know where I am with it. But I've never had black before except for evenings.'

'It's very nice,' Anna said, quite surprised. It made Jane look more statuesque than plump. 'I'll buy it for you if you're broke. I can get the cost back off my firm if I'm clever.' Jane looked as if she was going to cry at last, but in the end she cheered up and accepted. When they parted, she promised to look for Greg Morland's address. She seemed quite keen to land him in as much trouble as she could.

Chapter 26

Anna got off the bus and walked home. She was thinking how tough Jane Marshall was, and how she took bad news, and bought a dress, and decided how to shake her life back into shape. It helped that she thought her husband a bit of a heel at the best of times, and it helped that he had been away so long. But still, Jane was warm, tough, and practical. On first meeting her, Anna had thought her hard. But now she didn't. And even if it were so, a trace of flint was needed under the circumstances.

The black BMW was parked outside her door when she got home. At first she got the frisson she always experienced when she saw it unexpectedly. Then she remembered that there were ructions ahead and she had not prepared herself. So she walked round the block trying to achieve the proper state of mind. In some respects, Olsen always took her breath away and she wanted to be in control of herself for this meeting.

When she got back, the BMW was gone.

Selwyn said, 'You may well look like a wet Saturday; you just missed Charlie Blue Leader.' He never used Olsen's name when a soubriquet would do as well. 'He said meet him at eight in Thor's. And what did you mean by walking off and leaving that dreadful music thundering away? I knocked for hours.'

'On the ceiling, I suppose,' she said, annoyed. 'What else did he say?'

'And by the time I remembered the spare key, it'd switched its silly self off,' Selwyn said indignantly.

'Sorry,' Anna said, with a due show of penitence. 'Did he say anything else.'

'I should bloody well think so. You've no respect for the fragile nature of the creative urge.' Selwyn loved receiving apologies but he had no idea what to do with them. He said, 'I say, do you think I could come to supper with you? Bea's spending the night at her sister's.'

Anna stared firmly upstairs. She said, 'Not a good idea tonight.'

'Why not? The demon lover wouldn't mind. You've been living in each other's pockets for weeks now. He probably fancies a bit of intelligent conversation.'

'Honest, Selwyn,' Anna said, continuing on her way. 'You'd be de trop tonight, believe me.'

'God's teeth!' Selwyn yelled. 'If you can't tell a man he's not wanted in English, young Leo, it's time for a change of company for you too! Talk about pretentions.'

Selwyn, Anna thought, had an uncanny talent for tactlessness which left you speechless.

She showered and washed her hair, and took unusual care over dressing. Crunch time, she kept telling herself, better look your best. She was nervous. Selwyn's venerable school-

boy act had irritated her. Usually it was a source of amusement that he kept his sensitivity for his work but blundered
through life with the insight of a lawn mower. She tried to
concentrate on what she wanted to say this evening. But she
couldn't, and she blamed Selwyn.

It was nearly time to go when Jane Marshall phoned and
gave her Greg Morland's address. She said, 'If you do see
him, give him one in the goolies from me. 'Cos if I find out he
just left Edward out there to die, I'll bleeding do him. I swear
I will.'

'I'll see how it goes,' Anna said. She hadn't decided what
to do about Greg Morland yet. His address was in Westbury,
Wilshire and she did not want to go all the way out there
again. Not now, at any rate.

'And listen, thanks for everything, eh?' Jane mumbled
before she hung up. Anna couldn't think what she was being
thanked for. All she had done was find Edward's dead body
and that hardly called for gratitude, she thought bitterly. She
looked around for something she could potter with to delay
leaving. But there was nothing, so she locked the door and
went noisily downstairs. But Selwyn stayed in a huff behind
his door battering the ancient Olivetti. There was nothing left
but to go and meet Olsen.

Thor's was packed to the door with the rich and successful,
and with those who wanted to eat next to them. Winning and
dinning rather than wining and dining, Olsen had said once.

He was already there and stood up to attract her attention.
As she made her way over to him she tried to rid herself of
Olivia's words which had collected in her ear like poison. All
the same, it was not Ian Olsen she was greeting but Olivia's
husband.

'So,' he said, as they sat down, 'you've met Olivia. What did you think of her?'

Anna looked at him carefully, but his face was expressionless. She said, 'Formidable.' He smiled as if she had paid him a compliment. Her heart sank. He picked up the menu and said, 'I understand she told you about her situation.'

'What I can't understand,' she said, 'is why you didn't.'

'Yes,' he said thoughtfully. 'Well, I didn't want to spoil things between us until I knew if it was going to affect you one way or the other. Olivia, unfortunately, has no such scruples.' He sounded as if he admired Olivia's lack of scruples. A waiter appeared at his elbow and they ordered; he carefully, she at random. When the waiter left, she said, 'Well? How does it affect me?'

'First,' he said. 'I'd like to know how you see the problem.' He was being cagey, she thought angrily. He looked alert and interested but hardly as if what she had to say was important to him. She swallowed and said, 'Olivia has appointed you as daddy for her child. It's up to you to accept the post or not as you see fit.'

'As simple as that?'

'Don't ask me,' Anna said as calmly as she could. 'The most I know is that she didn't want you and I thought you wanted me. Now she wants you again. If that changes everything, you should say so.'

'Olivia has very powerful needs and desires,' Olsen said. 'How powerful are yours?'

'What's that got to do with it?' Anna said, hardly able to believe her ears. 'Is this some kind of wanting contest? You go to the highest bidder without showing any preference of your own?' The conversation had taken such an unexpected turn that she felt confused.

He said slowly, 'This is difficult to explain, but where Olivia is concerned I am often left without very much to say in the matter of my own preference.'

'You?' Anna said incredulously. The wine waiter arrived with a bottle, so she was forced to keep quiet until he had gone. When he had, Olsen said, 'Let us just say that perhaps Olivia and I are very much alike in that we are both attracted to power in each other. She only left me when it looked as though I was failing.'

'Very understandable,' Anna said flatly. Olsen smiled and there was a long pause. She was completely at a loss how she should proceed. She simply did not know what was required. After a while, the food came and Olsen began to eat. She picked up her fork, but as breathing seemed suddenly difficult and she wasn't hungry, she put it down again. Finally she said, 'I really don't understand. Are you saying that as Olivia wants you back that's the end? Or what?'

'It doesn't have to be like that,' he said, looking at her speculatively. 'You could fight.'

'I could fight?' Anna asked. It was like talking to a stranger.

'You have the advantage of youth,' he said musingly. 'Olivia's terrified of aging.'

'And where would you be all the while?' she said angrily. 'In your fall-out shelter waiting to be captured by the victor? Is this one of your games or something?'

'Of course it's a game,' Olsen said, suddenly bitter. 'Don't you know that by now? It's all a bloody game. That's why winning and losing's so important.'

Anna felt sick. She said, 'Well, it's not a bloody game to me.'

'I see,' he said quietly. 'I'm sorry.'

She wanted him to be as hurt as she was, but he only looked regretful. She wondered how long it would take to build a wall between what she had hoped for and the feeling of absolute rejection she had now. It seemed that she had wasted all her time and emotions on a shadow. She waited for him to say something else, but nothing came. In the end she said, 'Well, I think I'll go home now. I hope you'll be happy with whatever it is you've chosen to do, but I'm afraid I'm not playing.'

'You're probably very wise,' he said, taking her hand. 'I never meant this to happen.'

'But now that it has you won't do a damn thing to stop it.' She snatched her hand back. His touch made her want to cry and as she felt she had lost everything but her dignity the last thing she wanted was to break down in public.

She left. Out in the street, the air was cold and she could breathe again. She half wanted him to follow her, and hold her, and say he was sorry, but wanting comfort from the very person who is injuring you was an absurdity. So she turned towards the river and walked until her legs ached.

Chapter 27

She tried to walk upstairs without Selwyn hearing, but the staircase creaked like an out of tune piano and he burst out of his flat crying. 'What're you doing back so soon? Has Lord Tarquin recovered his sanity and chucked you out at last? I say, Leo, what's wrong?'

'Go away, Selwyn,' Anna said drearily. 'I think I've gone and done something I'm going to regret forever.'

'Then go and undo it,' Selwyn said, looking very concerned.

'I can't,' she said. 'And even if I could, I think I'd regret that just as long.'

'I'll get the bottle,' Selwyn said hurriedly. 'Don't cry, Leo. For God's sake don't cry till I've got the bottle.'

Later, when another bottle had somehow become empty, he said for the umpteenth time, 'He's mad or a masochist or both. And you're too bloody good for him.'

'No, no, no,' Anna said. 'He's wunnerful. It was me. I should've stuck to someone my own size, like you said.'

'No, no,' Selwyn said. 'He's mad. Mad and bad. And I'm

going to insist that . . . that . . . I don't know. You ought to go to bed. You're as drunk as a Scotsman on Cup Final night.' His eyelids fell like roller blinds and he started to snore. Anna heaved his legs on to the sofa and covered him with Bea's knitted lap rug. He looked like a crumpled baby. She patted his head fondly and tiptoed unsteadily up to bed.

She dreamed that Olsen was kneeling at her feet in the wet grass. 'Love me,' he pleaded. 'Fight for me.'

'No,' she answered, weeping.

'Fight for me,' he repeated. Still weeping, she kicked him hard and he fell over. She took her Swiss army knife out of her pocket and sawed off the leg she had kicked him with. He picked it up and left by the lychgate. The garden had become a cemetery.

Peering over the yew hedge, she saw him meet Olivia on the street outside. He gave her Anna's leg and she held it like a bouquet of flowers. They went into the Café Royal, hand in hand.

Anna sat on a gravestone and wondered if the leg would grow back. The epitaph on the gravestone read, 'Together in Eternity; Legless in Gaza.'

The verger appeared from the vault of a crypt. 'This place is only for the living,' he shouted. 'You're trespassing. It's a life sentence for what you've just done. No excuses now. You haven't a leg to stand on.'

'It'll grow back,' Anna screamed in panic, and woke up.

She was fully clothed and the bedside clock told her it was almost six-thirty. She was still slightly tipsy and felt as if she were falling.

By seven, she had bathed and changed and had made a pot of coffee. She stared out of the window while she drank. The street was granite grey. There were three more days of leave left and then the weekend. Five days seemed interminable. She put her mug down and went to the telephone.

Bernie said, 'What time is it, for God's sake?'

'Listen, Bernie, I'm going to Wiltshire to see a man about Edward Marshall.'

'Wait a minute,' Bernie said, yawning loudly. 'Don't do that. You're on leave and besides you're finished with Marshall.'

'Well, I'm going anyway. Sometimes the only course of action is action.'

There was a short silence and then Bernie said, 'What's up, love? Is anything the matter?'

'No,' Anna said, blinking rapidly. 'It's just that I'm tired of not having any say in what happens. I've got a good lead in Wiltshire and I know I can find out what happened to Marshall. I'm phoning you so that someone'll know where I've gone, that's all. But I'm going anyway.'

'All right,' Bernie said quickly. 'But come to breakfast first and we'll talk it over. Then if you're still set on going, I'm sure Syl will lend you her car.'

For the moment, Anna had forgotten about the Renault. The insurance claim had not been settled. So she agreed and rang off.

Syl was in the kitchen scrambling eggs and frying bread when Anna arrived. She poured her a glass of orange juice. The coffee was percolating and filled the room with a smoky breakfast smell. Bernie was still upstairs, shaving.

Anna sipped her juice and watched Syl cooking. She flipped the fried bread and stirred the eggs, always looking as if what she was doing was the most important thing in the world and she enjoyed doing it. Bernie had just the same characteristics. He too could look totally immersed in whatever he attended to. For a minute Anna considered this ability of couples to look like each other. Then a sensation of vertigo overtook her and she stopped thinking about it.

'Are you feeling all right?' Syl asked, lifting her eyes briefly from the eggs. 'Only you look as if you haven't slept. And your eyes are a bit red.'

'I'm fine,' Anna said, forcing a weak smile. 'But I went on a binge with Selwyn last night and Bea wasn't around to blow the whistle.'

Bernie came in knotting his tie and whistling 'I've Got You Under My Skin'. He hugged Syl and ruffled Anna's hair before sitting down. Syl dished up the eggs for Bernie and herself and poured coffee for all three of them. The light which had looked so grey in North Kensington filtered through the curtains and bathed the two of them in buttercup yellow. Anna got up and left the room. She sat on the downstairs lavatory for five minutes. Then she blew her nose and came out again.

'What's the story?' Bernie asked, wiping his mouth. Anna told him everything Jane Marshall had told her. 'She wants to know what happened,' she said at the end. 'I don't think anyone's going to tell her but me. The Met won't admit Marshall's whoever he was before he became Marshall. The local force don't know who he is because all his records must be under another name. So they can't even work through known associates and such. The Met won't help the locals. And Brierly Security wouldn't help a baby get its ball back unless it paid in advance. So as far as I can see, the body'll just stay in the meat safe with a question-mark on its identity bracelet for ever and ever amen. And Jane Marshall's left high and dry, not even sure if she's officially a widow.'

'Poor woman,' Syl said sympathetically. Bernie gave her a warning glance. He said mildly, 'Well, that's very noble of you, love, giving up your leave to help a poor widow. You realize, don't you, that even if you do wring some information out of this Greg Morland the Met can still smother it. Nobody has to tell you anything, you know. And whatever happens now, Jane Marshall's still a widow.'

'I can try,' Anna said stubbornly.

'I'm not stopping you,' Bernie said, sighing. 'Just so long as you're honest with yourself. Why you're doing it, I mean. And just so long as you ring me every night at seven. Because if you don't, I'll pull the rug so fast your eyes'll water.' He paused while Syl poured him some more coffee. Then he said, 'I don't know what's the matter with you and I'm not asking. But it doesn't look to me as if your judgement's too brilliant. That's why, if you're going, it's against my advice and that's why I want to know where you are and what you're up to.'

'Is that all?' Anna said sulkily.

'No. Whatever the outcome, you've got to promise you'll be back in the office Monday morning. Right?'

'*Jawohl, Herr Kapitän,*' Anna said flippantly. Bernie gave her a long hard look; so she pulled herself together and apologized.

She felt better when she was on the road. Syl's elderly but perfectly maintained Mini chugged along happily, and she could forget everything else and concentrate on her driving.

Chapter 28

She had left London at around nine and it was well before midday when she arrived in Westbury. She went straight to the address Jane Marshall had given her. It was an upstairs flat in a row of brick council houses on the edge of town.

The girl who opened the door looked like a pregnant schoolgirl. She had long thin hair and long thin legs. There were spots at the corners of her mouth and Anna noticed uneasily that one of the eyes peering at her from beneath a straggly fringe had been blackened lately. She said, 'Greg ain't home. I thought you was from the Council. There's damp and all that black stuff in the bathroom.'

'You want to leave a window open. It's not having proper ventilation makes black mould grow,' Anna said. The flat managed to be both cold and airless. It smelled of stale cigarette smoke. 'Where would I find Mr Morland at this time of day?'

'It's Thursday, ain't it? He'll be at the auction, like as not,' the girl said. 'I've tried leaving the window open, but the rain comes in and the sill's all rotten. The wind's from that side, see.'

The auction, when Anna found it, was on the other side of town. 'Turn right where all they Tesco lorries is,' the girl had told her. 'You can't miss it. It's got West Country Motor Auction written ever so big on the sheds.'

There were two sheds. One for cars worth more than five hundred pounds and the other for those worth less. Anna wandered in and out of both. There were a lot of people watching and bidding. Outside, the cars were lined up for the buyers to inspect before they were driven into the sheds. Crowds of men were looking under bonnets and into boots. Any one of them could have been Greg Moreland. She went over to the man on the gate and asked him. He said, 'Haven't seen him today. If he's here, he'll be over by the under five hundreds. Here, Walt,' he shouted to someone passing. 'Seen Greg Moreland?'

Walt said he was over by the under fives, wearing a black leather jacket, you couldn't miss him. Then he drew Anna aside, and said out of the corner of his mouth. 'Friend of yours? No? Well, I wouldn't buy anything off him if I was you. If you're after a nice little run-around, I've got just what you're looking for. One careful owner. Sweet as a nut.' He pressed a sticky business card into Anna's hand and said, 'Look me up any time. I'll see you right, nice girl like you. Don't you bother with the likes of him.'

Greg Morland had long black sideburns and the oily quiff that Anna had noticed before on a certain type of West Country man. He straightened up when he saw her approaching and said, 'Looking for me, doll?' He stuck his thumbs in his belt and twitched his pectorals. 'You want to check out the biceps, darlin', or was it business?' He grinned and rolled his cigarette from one corner of his mouth to the other. For Anna, it was loathing at first sight.

'In fact, business,' she said, trying not to let the coldness show.

'You want a motor? You want me to fix you up?' He leered. The accent was a peculiarly repulsive mixture of cowboy drawl and West Country.

'Not a motor, no.' A tall thin man unfolded himself from under the car they were standing near and blinked at her from behind thick spectacles. She looked at him and said, 'It's a bit confidential, really.'

'Don't worry about Keith,' Greg said. 'He's my partner.'

'In everything?' Anna said doubtfully. 'I told you it wasn't about motors.'

'I ride shotgun,' Keith said importantly. He looked a bit simple. Greg said, 'What's the pitch, doll?'

'Well, I met a man who said you knew a bit about hunting,' Anna said in a low voice, looking round furtively. 'Now, I'm representing a certain punter. No names. Let's just call him Ahmed. Know what I mean?' Greg nodded wisely and looked suitably intrigued.

'This Ahmed,' Anna went on, fighting down a sudden urge to burst out laughing, 'is the kind of guy willing to shell out a fair whack for his kicks. Understand?'

'I know the type,' Greg said, folding his arms and leaning back against the car. He was, Anna thought, definitely interested.

'I thought you might,' she said knowingly. 'I get a reasonable commission for making the right introductions.' And this contact of mine said you might be the right introduction.'

'Could be,' Greg said, showing his teeth. 'This Ahmed, what's he after, exactly?'

Anna looked quickly over her shoulder and said, 'The big one. Not Roe and not Fallow . . .'

'Red Deer,' Keith said excitedly. 'Greg's your man.'

'Shut up,' Greg said, not looking at all displeased.

'Also,' Anna went on in a whisper, 'this Ahmed, well, he's into unusual weapons.'

'Oh yeah?' Greg said, tough and confident. 'What kind?'

'The silent kind.'

'Say no more,' Greg said, winking at Keith. 'Well, I might be able to help you out, doll. Who'd you say your contact was?'

'I didn't,' Anna said. 'Let's just say it's someone I met in Bristol.'

'Must be Micky,' Keith said. 'We haven't seen him since . . .'

'Shut up!' Greg said. This time he looked genuinely annoyed. 'What else did Micky fucking Mouth say about me?' He glared suspiciously at Anna.

'Just if I was looking for something different in the way of, er, sport—you were a man who knew the ropes,' she said indifferently. 'If it's too much for you, say so now. Nothing lost. There's someone else I can approach.'

'Nothing's too much for me, doll,' Greg said, scowling and flexing his shoulders. 'I know where to find stag big enough to make this wog's eyes fall out. And I got weapons he's never heard of. What's it worth to him?'

'Not so fast. This is a deal that calls for mutual good faith. We're not talking about potting tin ducks at a fairground. My punter's a man with a position in society. I've got to be sure you're not stringing him along, or setting him up.'

'I wouldn't set him up,' Greg said indignantly. 'There's as much risk to me as there is to him. They don't exactly love poaching in this place I'm thinking of. What I want to know is, is he worth the risk?'

'He mentioned a grand for a good night out,' Anna said, almost laughing again. 'And a bit on top for a trophy.'

Keith whistled through his teeth. Greg said, 'Half now, half after?'

'Are you crazy?' Anna said, shocked. 'He may be foreign but he's not a moron. He'll want to see you first. He'll want to see the equipment. You've got to prove you can deliver.'

'Oh, I can deliver, darlin'.' Greg winked again. 'Just try me.'

'I can't wait,' Anna said, smiling unpleasantly. 'In the meantime, can we set up a meet? Somewhere quiet, where you can show Ahmed the terrain. And remember Ahmed's a shy geezer. In his position he's got to be.'

'Whatever you say, doll,' Greg said. 'And he'll bring half the lolly?'

'You get it when he's satisfied. Got a map?' Greg swaggered off to get one out of his car, leaving Anna with only Keith to think about. She stared at him until he blushed and looked at his shoes. After a moment, she said, 'I nearly didn't come. That Micky . . . what's his name . . .'

'Widowson,' Keith said awkwardly

'Yeah, him. He struck me as a bit of a loser. Does he always hang round the clubs?'

'Casinos mainly. Greg says it's a mug's game.' He stuck his thumbs in his belt in a weak imitation of his friend.

'Well, he wasn't winning the night we met him,' Anna said contemptuously. 'A place called the Golden Gate. Know it?'

Keith screwed his face up in a parody of thought and said, 'The one we used to go to was called the Century Club. Micky was a member. But we don't go no more now since Greg says Micky went soft.'

'Greg's right,' Anna said admiringly. 'You like hunting, don't you?'

'It's great. Like manoeuvres.'

'Were you in the Paras too?'

Keith blushed and said, 'I would've been if it wasn't for my eyes. There's lots of good men have bad eyes.'

Anna didn't reply. She had achieved almost everything she had come for and now she wanted to get away. There was an evil pleasure in manipulation; but it wasn't a pleasure she was proud of feeling.

Greg came back with a map and they arranged a rendez-vous for Friday night. Anna noticed that in picking a good spot, Greg gave the coombe where Marshall had died a wide berth.

Chapter 29

Bristol was not an easy place for a tired motorist unfamiliar with its eccentricities. It took Anna some time to get off the one way system and on to a street where she could park near a phone-box.

The name Widowson had not appeared on the Minehead hotel register. She looked it up in the directory. It was an unusual name and there was only one in the book. The address did not correspond to any in her notebook, but she found some change and rang the number anyway. After a while, a woman with a very educated accent answered. No, she did not know any Michael or Micky Widowson. Her husband's name was Matthew. Her daughter had been Widowson of course but now she was a Clarkson. First the son of a widow, then the son of a Clark. Funny, wasn't it? 'Especially if you were a daughter anyway,' Anna quipped and rang off thanking the woman.

She left the phone-box and stood by the car wondering what to do. The euphoria achieved by successfully kidding

Greg and Keith had dissipated. She was in a strange city a couple of hundreds miles from home and all she wanted to do was sleep. What she had done the night before had been more like stupor and only about five hours of it at that. The Olsens, giving her both barrels the previous day, had so interfered with mealtimes that she could not remember when she had last eaten. She could get a hotel room, she supposed, but as she was in Bristol at her own expense it did not seem worth while.

Sergeant Williams had to be brought up to date but she wanted to talk to Micky Widowson first. So there was nothing to do between now and phoning Bernie at seven. It would be several hours before the clubs and casinos began to open. So, Anna decided, first food and then, with luck, oblivion in the back seat of the Mini.

She awoke with a severe crick in the neck. It was almost exactly seven-thirty. Feeling unbalanced and other-worldly, she phoned Bernie and told him where she was, what she had done, and what she was going to do next. He said, 'Not bad, love. Quite sharp. I'm surprised really. I didn't think you could con a sick chicken the way you were this morning. But listen, you're not going anywhere near that meeting on Friday night, are you?'

'Not unless Sergeant Williams wants me there,' she said. 'Of course he may not be interested at all. In which case it's a wash-out.'

'Well, so long as we're agreed on that,' Bernie said. 'You should be all right with Widowson, because I agree with you, he must be the man with a conscience who sent you out to find Marshall. But will you ring me anyway, after you've found him? Doesn't matter what time. I just want to know you're still healthy.'

'Okay.'

'And you're starting tonight at the Century Club? All right. Well, good luck,' Bernie said. 'You can put a couple of quid on the black for me.'

'Not on your life,' Anna said. 'It's a mug's game. A mug just told me so this morning.'

She found the club in the basement of a large hotel near the centre of town. Sitting in the car watching the entrance, she saw that the clientele were predominantly Chinese and rather smart; jeans and a sweatshirt were not the thing at all. She collected her bag from the boot and marched smartly up the steps into the hotel. Fortunately, the lobby was busy so she followed the signs and discovered the ladies cloakroom close to the dining-room. She washed and changed in there, with her bag balanced on a convenient cistern.

It was not so simple at the Century Club. She had to part with a fiver to discover that Micky Widowson was still a member. But the man on the door either couldn't or wouldn't tell her if he was there. And she couldn't set foot in the club without becoming a member herself. As she counted out more money, she reflected that at this rate she wouldn't be able to afford more than a couple of wrong guesses. Perhaps Martin Brierly was right after all. One really did need a client to pick up the bills.

It was quiet downstairs and the tables were only thinly attended. She asked for Micky at the bar. He wasn't there, but the barman knew him and said he came in most nights. He promised to point him out when he did.

She ordered a lager and a steak sandwich and took them over to a booth. Nobody bothered her. Thinking about it, she realized that in all her years of being pestered by strange men, she had never been pestered by a Chinese. It would be a very restful world, she thought, if it were populated only by Chinese men. That was the last thing she remembered thinking before a touch on the shoulder woke her. The lager glass was empty, but the steak sandwich was cold and only half-eaten.

He was short and dark with curly hair and brown eyes. He said, 'I didn't mean to startle you, but they said you were looking for me.'

She looked at her watch and saw that she had been asleep for nearly three hours. The club was busy now and quite noisy. A waitress came over, laughing, and said, 'Some of the customers had bets you'd sleep through till closing time.'

'Was I snoring?' Anna asked, shamed. She ordered another lager and a Scotch and water for Micky. When the waitress had gone she said, 'I'm Anna Lee. I work for Brierly Security and it was me you sent out on the moor to find Edward Marshall. It was you that called, wasn't it?'

He stared at her for a moment and then to her horror he burst into tears. He put his head on his arms on the table between them and gave way completely.

The waitress came with the drinks while he was still in this position and Anna sent her away for more whiskey. She thought he would need more than one drink when he recovered from his tears.

After a while his shoulders stopped shaking, and he sat up blowing his nose. He said, 'I'm sorry. I haven't been able to talk about it to anyone.' His voice was thick and husky now, but she could recognize it as the one Beryl had recorded. She pushed his drink towards him, and he took half of it in one swallow.

'The chap at Vito's is a friend of mine,' he said, knuckling his eyes. 'He rang me up, and told me you'd been in asking for Ned. You left your card with him, see. That's how I got your number.' He finished his first drink and started on the second one.

'I saw a dead mule in Spain once,' he said, knocking back the whisky. He shuddered, whether from the whisky or from the dead mule Anna could not tell. But he did not pursue the subject. She called the waitress over again. Micky looked as if he needed a regular supply.

'It's like a romantic dream,' he said moodily. 'You go out at twilight—a few guys together, all tooled up—hunting, and you feel like nothing can touch you. Men must go to war feeling like that. The first time, anyway.'

Anna sipped her drink and let him talk. Sleeping at the wrong time of day made her brain shuffle badly. The relevant questions would come from listening, she hoped. He was an odd one, though. His sensitivity was contradicted by a broad, stocky frame. Perhaps he was one of those men with two vocabularies, a crude one for men and a softer one for women. Perhaps he could impress in both directions, but would become confused in mixed company.

'Greg had done the scouting,' he was saying. 'And he said there was stag down there. We fanned out and went down the hill, very quiet, like.'

Not the way Flora told it, Anna recalled. She said nothing.

'Greg went round the other side of a small hill and we got separated—Greg and Keith on one side—me and Ned on the other. Ned was between me and Greg. The idea was to stalk the stag down in the bottom of the coombe and then beat them up to where the bank was steep—where we could get a clear shot in.' He paused and rubbed his forehead distractedly. 'We never got down to the bottom, though,' he said. 'When we crept round the bluff, it happened. You don't hear much from a crossbow, but it was very quiet there. I could tell someone had loosed off a shot. Ned screamed. You never heard anything like it. I just stood there. I couldn't move—I tell you—I just could not move. You won't believe me, but it's true.'

'I believe you,' Anna said reassuringly. She was afraid he was going to cry again. But he didn't. He said, 'You think about it sometimes, what you'd do in an emergency. I always saw myself going into action all calm and resourceful, like. That's a laugh. I could hear Keith yelling, 'You hit him. You killed him.'' Something like that. And Greg shutting him up.'

He stopped for another swallow. 'I didn't panic, like Keith did. Nothing like that. I just sort of went numb. Sort of zombie-like. I thought, if I thought anything, that Greg'd know what to do. He'd been in the army too, you know. And they're trained for things like that. He said, "He's dead. We'd better get out of here." So I went. Just like that. Because Greg said so. I never even went over to Ned to see for myself. I never told them we ought to get him back to the road. Nothing. Greg said go, and I went. Just like that. I still can't believe it.

'I mean, as we were climbing back up the hill, I even thought I heard Ned calling. But Greg said it was an owl. I know it wasn't a bloody owl. But whatever Greg said was all right by me.

'Keith was squawking like a frightened hen. I didn't do that. But in the end, what I did was bloody worse. I did nothing. I was like a dead man walking up that hill. Deader than Ned.'

Chapter 30

A commotion was bubbling up at one of the green baize tables. Someone apparently was having some good fortune. Micky turned his head to see what was going on, and the spell was broken. He cleared his throat and said formally, 'I'm sorry to go on about it. Something happened to me, you see . . .'

'And you've never felt the same about yourself,' Anna supplied after a lengthy pause. 'I know. It's happened to me too.' It was time to take charge of the conversation, to steer him back to the fundamental questions. Or, having confessed his suppressed guilt, he would leave her with it and go on his way, feeling better but without anything of value having been accomplished. She asked, 'How long have you known Ned?'

He looked at her, rather strangely, she thought. So she said, 'Look, there's a question in the back of my mind. And that is was Ned's death an accident?'

'Of course it was an accident,' he said, outraged. 'What're you talking about?'

'Well,' she said slowly, 'someone was looking for Ned. I know that for a fact. I'll tell you about it if you'll tell me everything about him first. He wasn't Edward Marshall, was he?'

'No.' He rested his head in his hands and thought about it for a long time. Anna left him think. He would either tell her or he wouldn't. She couldn't force him. In the end he said, 'No. He was born Edward Widowson. He's my brother.'

That was the last thing Anna had expected to hear. Her mouth was hanging open, so she shut it and said, 'Yes?' hoping she did not sound as astonished as she was.

'But I still don't know why he's like he is. Was.'

As is usual with close relatives, Micky talking about Ned was Micky talking about himself. Like brothers and sisters everywhere, he could not take Ned at his own value—as a unique personality. Rather, his story was a series of comparisons between the two of them.

Micky was younger by a year. Ned had been the more physical of the two. Micky, the brighter, had been the parents' favourite. He had overtaken his brother at school. There followed a period of bitter resentment. The brothers scarcely spoke, and then only to fight. Ned left school under a cloud. Micky worked hard and achieved some respectable results. Micky was bettering himself. Ned was going to the dogs.

It was something about a gang breaking into a warehouse. Ned was never charged but a severe warning from the police resulted. There was a family crisis. No one had been in trouble before. Fur flew, and finally Ned decamped and joined the army. He was just eighteen. Surprisingly, he made a success of it and was accepted into the Paras. He stayed for seven years.

Meanwhile, Micky went to technical college to do engineering and later got a good job at Westland Helicopters. The family star was rising. The brothers were friendlier than they had ever been before.

While he was in the army, Ned met and married Jane. Micky had gone to London for the wedding with Greg and some other Bristol cronies. That was the first time he saw her, and he had loved her ever since.

'She didn't like me much, though,' he said mournfully. 'It was that bloody Greg again, see. She tarred us with the same brush.'

'Ned's stag night?' Anna asked.

'It was pretty disgusting,' Micky admitted soberly. 'Ned didn't seem to mind, though. She was too good for him by half.'

All this had taken some time. Anna was tired. The question of who and where was Mr Thurman remained outstanding. She said, 'What happened after the army? How did Ned get into trouble again?'

'I honestly don't know,' Micky said, rubbing his eyes. He looked exhausted. 'It must be something that's in him. He was very let down after the army. Couldn't find anything that suited. He said the army'd only taught him to jump out of airplanes and there wasn't much call for that in Civvy Street. But if you ask me, it was the company he missed—the boys. That, and always having something to do.'

Anna thought about this and about the Paras. They were an exclusive regiment. Perhaps Ned had needed that peculiar combination of security, adventure, and superiority. She had noticed the same combination in some criminal families.

Anyway, Micky told her, it was not long before Ned was arrested and subsequently imprisoned for drug-smuggling. Micky kept in touch, largely, Anna guessed, because he wanted to help Jane. To his sorrow, though, Jane neither wanted nor needed help and kept him at arm's length.

When Ned got out of prison, he found a job driving tankers all over Europe. Micky saw him now and then. There were occasional hunting trips with the boys, occasional weekends in London for Micky. He thought Ned had pulled himself together. He was altogether more collected, more like the soldier he had been.

When the crash came, it was a big one. Ned was again charged with drugs offences, but this time an entire organization was pulled in. It seemed that the investigation had started with the discovery of a corpse: a courier for a drug ring. Micky wasn't too sure about that, but it had led, eventually, to Ned's arrest along with many others. The sentences ranged from ten to twenty years. Ned got fourteen.

Micky had not attended the trial. What with the publicity and everything, the family had come under great pressure. His mother became ill and finally died of a stroke.

'My dad's never forgiven Ned,' Micky said. 'He doesn't even talk about him. In fact, he thinks he's still in prison.'

'How long did he actually do?' Anna asked.

'Only two years,' he said, as if the memory still perplexed him. 'You could've knocked me down with a feather. He rung me up at work one day, about two years ago. Could we meet for a drink? I'd no idea he was out. So we met, and he said he shouldn't rightly be seeing me. He'd got another name, he said. It was a fresh start and he didn't want anyone to know who he was. So 'course I swore I wouldn't let on.

'Well, he managed to keep his head down for a couple of months, and then I suppose he got bored. It wouldn't hurt to swear old Greg in and get in a bit of hunting, he said. So we started going out again and that was that.'

Anna said, 'Was Greg involved in this drugs thing?'

'Not a chance.'

'How do you know?'

Micky shook his head. He had been drinking steadily and was now quite flushed. Sweat stood out on his brow. 'He didn't know anything about it till it was in the papers. He rung me up and said had I seen. He thought it made Ned a big man. Berk, huh?'

'Yeah,' Anna said absently. It didn't prove anything. Micky obviously knew little about the drugs or the trial, but nevertheless she asked if he knew Mr Thurman. He didn't. There didn't seem much point in asking him anything else. It would all be on public record anyway.

'What about Jane?' Micky said suddenly, staring intently at her. 'You've seen her. How is she? I wanted to go there but I couldn't face her. Do you think she'd see me now that it's all cleared up?'

He was really quite drunk. Anna said, 'But it isn't all cleared up. She knows Ned's probably dead, but only because I told her. His body still hasn't been identified because of the confusion of names. She already thinks Greg's in some way to blame, because of the hunting. But she can't do anything about it. Can she?'

'I'm a rotten bastard,' Micky said unexpectedly. 'A coward and a bastard. What am I going to do?'

Chapter 31

Anna woke at about ten-thirty. She had returned home at three and was still tired. On the whole she was glad; there were worse things to feel than tired. Things to be avoided. The sun was shining, but there was no heart in it.

The doorbell rang. She threw on jeans and a T-shirt, and ran downstairs barefoot to find Bernie on the doorstep. A lean and shabby cat dodged past him and ran up the stairs in front of them. The cat belonged to no one but was an occasional visitor to Anna. Selwyn called it Pillow Stuffer because when it could, on cold days, it brought stunned pigeons indoors to kill and eat, leaving piles of bloodstained feathers for Anna or Bea to sweep up.

'First the cat, then coffee,' Anna said, opening the fridge. Milk and an old pork chop, way past its prime, did for Pillow Stuffer. Bernie said, 'Have you rung Sergeant Williams yet?'

'No,' Anna said. 'It was too late when I finished last night.'

He accepted his coffee and said, 'I was thinking: why don't I talk to him for you?'

'That mightn't be a bad idea,' Anna said thoughtfully. 'He doesn't take me very seriously.'

'I'm supposed to be off to Basildon to see if some firm can identify a bag of polystyrene granules—Virgin Popcorn, it's called. You could do that instead.'

He wanted to make sure she didn't go back to Somerset and get into trouble, she thought. He was wearing his Uncle Bernie expression. Perhaps he had spoken to Selwyn.

'All right,' she said, grinning. 'Let's swap notes.'

Later that afternoon, at Bernie's house, they exchanged information again. For Anna's part the firm in Basildon had given an equivocal answer. They did make granules exactly like her sample; but so did three other firms. They needed to see the packaging to be sure.

Bernie's news was more positive. Sergeant Williams thanked her for the information. Bristol Headquarters would send someone round to take Micky's statement. He would probably have to identify Edward's body, if that were still possible. And someone would be there to meet Greg Morland at the rendezvous on the moor. He didn't think much of her methods, but he was going to make use of them. He did not want to see her anywhere near Exmoor till he'd got his results. Bernie repeated that part of the message twice. The protection racket was working well.

Anna smiled and said, 'Well, that's all in hand, then. Thanks very much. Bernie. Now there's only the question of Mr Thurman.'

'Oh no,' Bernie said decidedly. 'I've gone along with you

so far. But Mr Thurman is too far. That's a completely different pit of snakes and I'm not having it.'

'What do you mean, you're not having it?' Anna said with sudden anger. 'What's it got to do with you anyway? Mr Thurman made a Charley out of me. I was supposed to find Marshall so that he could take his name out of the phone book for him. That's a liberty.'

Syl looked round the kitchen door and said, 'Tea, anyone?'

'Lovely, Syl,' Bernie said, not taking his eyes off Anna. 'He made a Charley out of Mr Brierly. That's the old man's job, sorting out clients. It's him that slipped up, not you. You're just taking it personally for reasons of your own.'

'You've been talking to Selwyn,' Anna said, getting up, ready to stalk out of the house.'

'Mr Price has been talking to me,' Bernie corrected calmly. 'He couldn't find you when he woke up yesterday morning. So he thought you'd gone head first off Battersea Bridge or something silly like that.'

'He thinks everyone's as neurotic as he is,' Anna said, knowing as she said it how unfair she sounded.

'He's very fond of you,' Syl said sharply. 'You seem to think everyone's unreasonable except you. Well, it seems quite reasonable to be worried about you the way you acted yesterday.' It was like being stung by a butterfly. Anna sat down again. Bernie said, 'Look, you've shaken Greg Morland out of his tree and you've got Micky Whatsisname spilling his guts. It looks to me like displaced revenge for something else, but that's all right. If, however, you go on to stir up Mr Thurman, that's as good as going head first off Battersea Bridge. That's topping yourself because you fell for the wrong man. And that's bloody stupid.'

Anna thought about it while Syl made the tea. In the end, she said, 'Oh well, I suppose you've got a point. I'm sorry.'

It was going on for six o'clock and the traffic was heavy, so she stopped off in Kilburn. Jane opened the door looking pink and windswept. She said 'Hello, ducks, I'm glad you came by. Well, sort of. There's someone here I want you to meet.'

Anna followed her into the living-room and caught Yellow Fang in the act of putting his shoes on. He looked rather pink and windswept too.

'This is Ginger,' Jane said, and went to get beer and glasses from the sideboard.

Ginger said, 'Oh no, not you again. We was beginning to call you Super Glue, my mate and me. I'm sorry about your motor, by the way. Only you shouldn't try and do handbrake turns in a Renault 4. You got to have the handbrake attached to the back wheels, see.'

'I thought about that,' Anna said, grinning warily. 'I thought about it all the way over the edge of the road.'

'Yeah, well, you wasn't hurt, was you?' Ginger said, pouring beer into his glass, and a drop for the carpet too. 'We only wanted a word, my mate and me. You could get killed, overreacting like that.'

'I seem to remember, last time we met, you said my days were numbered anyway.'

'Yeah, well, that's what we was there for, wunnit? Making sure no one bothered Janey here.' He grinned. 'We might've got a bit enthusiastic, but no harm done.'

'What happened in Westbury?' Jane asked. Anna looked at Ginger and then back at Jane.

'Oh, don't worry about Ginge,' Jane said, plonking herself down next to him, making the sofa bounce. 'We sort of got together Tuesday night and everything's okay now.' They held hands and looked very okay indeed. So Anna told them about the trap waiting for Greg Morland.

'Strewth,' Ginger said. 'I'd lose my stripes doing what you did. Still, I hope they nail the little sod.'

'Wish I could see it,' Jane said seriously.

Anna did not tell her about Micky. Micky had troubles enough already. Instead, she told Ginger about Mr Thurman. He said, 'I was going to ask you about that. Because it doesn't seem Edward's cover was watertight, does it? I mean, that's got to be looked at, hasn't it?'

'That's up to you,' Anna said. It was as far as she could go without breaking her promise to Bernie. 'But if you've got any more informers under wraps who've only done two years I'd watch them pretty carefully if I were you.'

Ginger didn't say anything, but he looked thoughtful.

Chapter 32

If Anna had wished for the affair to be settled by one positive action of her own, she was disappointed. She eventually heard that Greg Morland had been arrested on the Friday night. The news took days to reach her and even then it was at third hand. But that was the nature of her job: to paddle on the edge of other people's dramas, usually long after they had lost significance to the major participants. Already she had taken her part in it further than her job allowed and if she was not satisfied with the results it was through no fault of hers. It was the way of things. And now it was over.

She went back to work on Monday and began a stint for a finance company tracing bad debtors. After that, she was hired by a small chain of boutiques to advise on theft prevention. And still later, she found herself lurking in doorways late at night, attempting to discover which of a disco's employees was stealing cigarettes and alcohol.

Towards the end of this job Anna caught a dose of flu which laid her up, weak and feverish, racked by a violent cough, for nearly two weeks. For a while, she was sustained by Bea's chicken soup. But when Bea too succumbed to the bug, they were both rather less well sustained by Selwyn's takeaway pizza. Selwyn did not catch flu, although he tried very hard. It was not his role, he felt, to bring comfort or take-away pizza to the sick. The sick should comfort him. And they often had to, as he grumbled and complained far more than they did.

Anna was very uncomfortable. Between coughing fits she slept badly and woke sweating and shivering with pain exploding in her head and chest. Sometimes she dreamed. Mostly she dreamed she was on Exmoor looking for a man. Instead of one, she found two and they were both dead. She was very depressed.

One day Selwyn brought up visitors. It was Jane and Ginger.

'Farkinell, look at you,' Jane said cheerfully. 'You look like something the sausage factory turned down. Where do you keep the clean sheets? Here, Ginge, give us a hand with this bed. She's been plaiting ropes with them sheets.'

Anna sat in a chair by the fire while Jane and Ginger made sense of her tangled bed. Then she had a wash and changed into clean pyjamas. It was a great improvement.

'Have you seen the papers?' Ginger asked, when she was settled more or less comfortably. A great improvement had come over him too. He had even had his teeth scaled and the result was quite striking.

'If you haven't,' he went on, 'you won't know; but we've had a nasty bit of doings up in Hertfordshire. It could be your Mr Thurman's been naughty again.'

'How come?' Anna croaked.

'I'm not supposed to tell you this,' he said, giving her a

foxy smile. 'But seeing as you've been good to Janey here, I don't mind saying you was right. We did have another informant in mothballs. Well, we had to be cagey, didn't we? The whole frak-arse started with someone knocking off a courier, didn't it?'

'I suppose so,' Anna said wearily. It all seemed so long ago.

'Well anyway, this bleeding idiot was a bit like Edward: he couldn't keep away from his old mates. You do your best for them, see, but they won't listen, will they?' Ginger lit a cigarette and blew a long stream of smoke under Anna's nose. Jane took it away from him and when Anna had stopped coughing he said, 'Well, the long and short of it is that about three weeks ago there's some geezer walking his dog up near Welwyn. And the dog goes rooting around under some brambles and comes back with this hand, see, cut off at the wrist. 'Course the chap almost goes bonkers.'

'Amazing,' Jane said laconically.

'All right.' Ginger grinned sheepishly. 'Anyway, they're still looking for the rest of him, but we got some partial prints of the hand and, surprise, surprise, it's our bleeding idiot we thought was all safe and sound.'

'That's three down,' Anna said. 'Any more to go?'

'Two really,' Ginger corrected her. 'We're not counting Edward. Although we might have had to if he hadn't've had that accident first. It must be a big organization your Mr Thurman works for. Bigger than we thought. I mean, we thought we had everything sewn up, obviously.'

'Obviously,' Anna said weakly.

'But they're probably trading again. If they weren't, your Mr Thurman'd hardly bother going round discouraging talkers. You don't do that just for giggles.'

'Do you know who he is?'

'Not really,' Ginger admitted, 'but there's someone very like him been seen in Hong Kong. And we've had another report that tallied from Sydney. It seems everyone's looking. Someone'll pin him down someday, you'll see.'

But that was the last she ever heard.

She never saw Ian Olsen again either, although his name cropped up in the papers once or twice. In June he sent her a ticket for the semi-finals at Wimbledon. She went, but he wasn't there. She wrote to him several times after that, but the letters are still in the bottom drawer of her desk.

ABOUT THE AUTHOR

LIZA CODY is a graphic artist and novelist who lives in Frome, a small English village. Her first novel, *Dupe*, was nominated for the 1981 Edgar Award for best mystery of the year and won the John Creasey Award for the best first mystery published in England during 1980. Her other Anna Lee novels are *Bad Company*, *Stalker*, *Under Contract*, and *Head Case*.

HEAD CASE

Liza Cody

Young, attractive and tough, Anna Lee, Brierly Security's youngest agent, brings to her cases intelligence, courage and a fine instinct for ferreting out the often surprising truth. In HEAD CASE, Anna Lee finds herself searching for Thea Hahn, a girl described as brilliant, polite, quiet and neat—the kind of girl who has never given trouble to anyone. But as she begins to probe this extraordinary girl's past, Anna uncovers shocking contradictions. Perhaps Thea was more complex than she seemed.

CHAPTER 1

The morning began with a small domestic theft. Anna would have called it a loan but Selwyn was quite adamant.

'Don't, don't, don't take my morning paper!' he had bellowed after a previous infraction. 'And don't tell me you haven't. I always know. You steal the print off the page, the power from the words. And besides, you fold it up again all wrong.'

'What a fuss,' Bea said, all wifely contempt.

'You'll never understand.' Selwyn met contempt with disdain. 'It's my paper, and it's fresh and crisp I want it, with the smell of ink intact. Not after her upstairs has read the new off the news.'

Upstairs, right above Selwyn's sleeping head, Anna pilfered the news from the *Guardian*: there would be no peace summit, the social workers were threatening industrial action, the miners were already committing it, an old war hero was convicted of shoplifting, and Somerset were all out for 173. She poured another cup of coffee. Outside, the plane tree was beginning to darken into its dignified summer green and the daisies on the patch of grass looked in need of beheading.

Anna refolded the paper with great care. It did not look second-hand. She hoped Selwyn would never know, although he had an uncommonly sensitive nose for the unlikeliest things.

The new yellow client folder caught her eye. It contained a single sheet of paper: a Brierly Security interview form. Subject—Thea Hahn. Client—Mr Rodney Hahn, civil servant, married. An address in Wimbledon. A paragraph followed describing a telephone conversation between Rodney Hahn and Martin Brierly. Anna did not read it. She had already been told. Instead she gave her shoes a quick rub with a piece of Kleenex and checked her stockings for holes. She looked as neat and reliable as a representative of Brierly Security should when calling on a civil servant in Wimbledon.

Collecting bags, keys and *Guardian*, she blew a soft raspberry at the mirror and left the flat. She ran swiftly downstairs and out through the front door. There was no sign of Bea or Selwyn but it would never do to loiter in the hall in possession of a borrowed *Guardian*. Safely outside, she pushed the paper through the letter-box and left it at the rakish angle favoured by the paperboy.

It was already warm inside the car. There was a faint smell of plastic and axle grease. She rolled down the window, noted the mileage and turned on the radio. The Everly Brothers sang 'Crying in the Rain' as she drove through sunny, early morning streets to Hammersmith Bridge.

The river already had a steamy, glassy sheen to it. It was going to be another scorcher. The traffic had not yet coagulated into rush hour, and most of it was coming in the opposite direction. Anna made it to Wimbledon in good time.

Ansel Grove was leafy, with big houses set well back from the road and protected by high hedges. Mr Hahn's was hidden behind years of laurel growth and his lilacs were beginning to turn rusty at the edges. It was a low white house with the curved windows that always reminded Anna of school swimming pools.

She parked by the front door to avoid blocking the garage. A man appeared on the front doorstep just as she was getting out of the car. He looked at his watch.

'Right on time,' he said, as if congratulating her on a difficult feat. 'I'm Rodney Hahn.'

'Anna Lee. Good morning.'

He extended a creamy manicured hand and looked her over with sharp pale blue eyes. Anna shook the hand, hoping he wasn't going to say he had expected an older man.

'I was expecting someone older,' he said, holding her hand a fraction too long. 'Mr Brierly assured me all his agents were very experienced.'

'It's just the way I look,' Anna said.

'Well, come through anyway,' he said briskly. 'We're having breakfast on the terrace.'

He led the way into a wide hall with a terracotta tiled floor, through a shining regimented dining-room to the French windows which opened on to the back garden.

The remains of breakfast for two, pieces of croissant and eggy plates, lay on a white metal table. There were three chairs, though, and a third clean cup.

'Coffee?' Mr Hahn asked. 'Do sit. My wife will be down shortly.'

He picked up a deep-necked, bell-bottomed coffee pot and poured some weak, tepid coffee.

'Wonderful,' Anna lied gamely, studying him over the rim of her cup: tall, good-looking, beginning to grey in all the right places, well-cut sober suit, no skin showing between silk sock and trouser bottom. He was watching her too, a closed confident look with the beginning of a smile round his mouth.

He's going to tell me how he's never had dealings with a detective before, Anna thought, putting her cup down and getting ready to make a good impression.

'I've never actually employed a private detective before,' he said, the smile breaking through as though he should be applauded for the absence of necessity.

At that moment, Mrs Hahn appeared from the house. Anna stood up and was introduced. Mrs Hahn was wrapped in peach-coloured silk and Mitsouko. Her hair was gilded, her nails tinted and her long slim shins looked French-polished.

'Do forgive the godforsaken hour,' she murmured. 'Rodney so much wanted to see you himself, and before work is the most convenient time.'

'Meetings and so forth,' Mr Hahn supplied vaguely. 'One's colleagues can go on rather.'

Anna was rather overwhelmed by the picture of tasteful wealth the pair presented. Either Mr Hahn was a very superior civil servant, or someone had inherited something. She cleared her throat and said, 'Well now, about your daughter . . .'

'Yes,' Mr Hahn interrupted quickly. 'Thea. You see, I don't think the police really know what they're talking about.'

'Who they're talking to, actually,' Mrs Hahn put in. 'Do you know, they suggested we contact the Salvation Army?'

'The Salvation Army are very good,' Anna said.

'Yes, but with drunks and dropouts,' Mrs Hahn said. 'Of course, I won't hear a word against them, but there's no reason in the world why Thea should go to them.'

'She's quite young, isn't she?' Anna said, knowing full well how old she was, but wanting the parents to start talking about her.

'Just sixteen,' Mr Hahn said. 'Valerie, have you sorted out the photographs? Mr Brierly said she would need photographs.'

'In the study, dear.' Mrs Hahn waved an immaculate hand, presumably in that direction. 'And while you're up, would you ask Mrs Elder for more coffee? This must be undrinkable.'

Mr Hahn went into the house, and Anna wondered which of this smooth couple called the tune. Mrs Hahn seemed quite content to wait until her husband returned, so Anna said, 'Thea's been gone for eleven days now. Would you tell me what steps you've already taken?'

'Well, the police, naturally,' Mrs Hahn said, turning her face up towards the morning sun and closing her eyes. No breeze stirred the garden: leaves and blossom hung motionless. She took a pair of sunglasses out of her silk wrap pocket and put them on.

'Thea was lodging with a cousin, at the time,' she went on. 'Danielle Soper. You'll probably want to talk to her yourself. I've included a short list of relevant names and addresses in the envelope of photographs. I thought it might save time.'

'Thank you,' Anna murmured. 'Does Thea's cousin live near Thea's school, or what?'

'Ah, well. Thea doesn't actually go to school,' Mrs Hahn said, still giving most of her attention to the sun.

'Didn't my husband explain that to Mr Brierly? No? Well, Thea was attending some lectures at the University of London, and private tutorials.'

'I suppose one should describe Thea as gifted,' Rodney Hahn said, returning through the French windows. He placed a thick white envelope on the table. 'Her subject, basically, is mathematics. She could have begun at Cambridge last September, but neither we nor the authorities there thought it advisable. So she has been rounding out her education, so to speak, as a sort of external student at London.'

'Oh,' said Anna, rather flummoxed. 'I had no idea.'

'It would have been a somewhat complicated phenomenon to describe over the telephone,' Mr Hahn said coolly, 'besides being irrelevant to the circumstances. Our daughter is not some sort of freak, as we take great pains to point out to anyone who might be overly impressed with her academic achievements.'

'Of course,' Anna said, feeling as if she were consoling him for a hardship. Perhaps having an exceptionally clever child was a hardship, although most of the parents she knew complained about the opposite.

'Ah, coffee,' Mrs Hahn said with evident relief. 'Thank you, Mrs Elder.'

Mrs Elder, a more motherly-looking figure than Mrs Hahn, put a pot of fresh coffee on the table, nodded good morning to Anna, and left without a word. Mr Hahn poured for Anna and Mrs Hahn. His own cup stayed empty. He looked at his watch.

Anna said quickly, 'So what steps have you taken in the last eleven days?'

'It has, in fact, been far less than eleven days,' Mr Hahn said. 'We only came to the conclusion that Thea was missing last Thursday.'

'Mrs Soper thought she was with us,' Mrs Hahn put

in. 'While we, of course, assumed she was still with Mrs Soper. It was only when Danielle phoned to ask why she had not returned for her Thursday lecture that we realized there was a problem.'

'We contacted the police immediately,' Mr Hahn said, again looking at his watch. 'And to cut a long story short, between their inquiries and Mrs Soper's, it is generally agreed that Thea has not been seen by anyone who knows her since Thursday, eleven days ago. Now, I'm afraid I must leave you.' He stood up.

Anna stared at him in surprise. She said, 'There are two broad categories for missing people. Those who want to be missing and those who don't.'

'I hope you aren't suggesting that Thea would put us to this trouble voluntarily,' Mrs Hahn said coldly, while Mr Hahn said, 'Yes, I see what you mean, but as I can think of no reason why she might wish to absent herself, I have no suggestion to offer.'

Anna could not ruffle him or detain him. He aimed a kiss at Mrs Hahn's perfect cheek and left. Anna said, 'I didn't mean to upset you. It's just that sometimes kids go off for reasons that the rest of us wouldn't understand at all.'

'You haven't upset me in the least,' Mrs Hahn said calmly. 'And, as I pointed out to the police, it would be a mistake to assume that Thea is one of those disaffected dropout teenagers.'

'So you think something must've happened to her?'

'If that is the only alternative to the first of your "broad categories", yes.' A well-bred hint of sarcasm was unmistakable. Anna felt the first trickle of sweat down her spine. She shifted uncomfortably. Mrs Hahn almost smiled.

To change the subject, Anna said, 'How long has Mrs Elder been with you?' hoping to find someone in this elevated household she could talk to on her own level.

'About ten years, I suppose. Why?'

'I'd like to talk to anyone who's involved.'

'Mrs Elder is not involved,' Mrs Hahn said flatly. 'However, if you think it might help . . .'

'And I'd like to look at Thea's room.'

'Very well.' Mrs Hahn stood up and led the way through the house. At the top of the stairs she paused and said, 'Since interviewing one's employees seems to be on your list of necessities, I should mention that my charwoman is coming at nine. She is not involved at all and I would be most displeased if you spoke to her. She does not yet know of Thea's disappearance, and I will not have family matters turned into neighbourhood gossip.'

'She works for your neighbours too?' Anna asked, almost smiling in her turn. It was nice to see Mrs Hahn's complacency slip, if only by a fraction. 'How about Mrs Elder?'

'Mrs Elder lives in,' Mrs Hahn said stiffly. 'I'll send her up. This is Thea's room.' She opened a door that led off the hall at the top of the stairs. Anna went in alone.

CHAPTER 2

Thea's room was painted a quiet grey-green—the sort of colour a decorator would call 'pussy willow'. Against one wall stood a narrow bed, with antique brass bedrails, covered by a white crocheted cover. There was a large desk under the window, and a reproduction of Rembrandt's son Titus over the bed. Apart from a built-in cupboard and wardrobe, the rest of the wall space was taken up by bookshelves.

Thea had at her disposal a complete set of *Encyclopædia Britannica*, Dickens, Scott, Hardy, Eliot, Austen and the Brontës; and that was only the light reading. There were volumes by Kierkegaard, Popper, Russell, Locke, Hobbes. The closest thing to a comic was *Scientific American*. There were books about physics, metaphysics, geophysics, astrophysics, astronomy, and mathematics.

Anna gulped and opened the cupboard where she was reassured to find an array of ordinary clothes. She was relieved to see that the only hat present would fit a normal-sized head. The cupboard, in fact, was remarkable for what it did not contain. There were no jeans, for instance, nothing made of denim—no T-shirts with writing on them, no sweatshirts, no trainers. Nothing that a sixteen-year-old, of the sort Anna knew, would choose. Everything looked conservative and tasteful and everything was made from natural fibres. They were all the sort of garments Mrs Hahn might have chosen.

Anna felt it was time to look at the head that wore the normal-sized hat. She was having difficulty imagining a young girl who had read all those intimidating books and unresistingly wore nice white cotton blouses and plaid woollen skirts.

She sat at the desk and tipped the photos out of the envelope.

The one on top of the small pile was a black and white studio portrait. The head was carefully halated, light catching hair, eyelids, and eyes—dark hair cut in a short, glossy page-boy, clear eyes, broad cheekbones, straight nose—a still, classical pose to a quiet, classical head. Only the mouth had a childish, indecisive look. It was the sort of photograph Thea's father might have in a silver frame on his office desk.

Anna sorted through the rest, trying to find one that showed Thea relaxed, unposed, or off-guard. Nothing. She stood between her parents in front of a rhododendron bush. She sat on the terrace in the garden with a book. She knelt on the grass with a spaniel she did not touch and which was anyway looking in the other direction.

'Mrs Hahn said you wanted a word,' Mrs Elder said from the doorway. Anna swung round. She asked impulsively, 'Which of these pictures would you say looks most like Thea?'

Mrs Elder came across the room, round and short-legged on neat little feet. She looked over Anna's shoulder. After a pause she said, 'Her father always liked that one best,' pointing to the studio portrait.

'And you?'

'Oh, it's very like her,' Mrs Elder said noncommittally.

'Yes, but what's she really like?'

Mrs Elder smiled and said, 'Oh, she's a lovely girl—so clever, very polite. She never gives anyone any trouble.'

'There's trouble now,' Anna said, quite sharp in her disappointment.

'Poor girl,' Mrs Elder said. 'I wonder what can have happened. I've never known the Hahns so upset.'

'But was she unhappy or something?' Anna asked bluntly. 'Could she have run away?'

'Oh no,' Mrs Elder said disapprovingly. 'She'd never give us any trouble like that.'

When Mrs Elder left her alone, Anna looked at the list of names and addresses Mrs Hahn had provided. There were only four, with Mrs Danielle Soper's at the top. Anna made a note to ask about old school friends. Thea must have gone to school at some point. Then she started opening desk drawers. By now she was not expecting to find any girlish secrets.

Downstairs, she heard the front door open and close, and after a while, the steady drone of a vacuum cleaner. She listened to the ordinary sounds almost with pleasure. She had found nothing she could understand in the desk: notebooks filled with figures and symbols, computer printouts, ring files filled with pages of incomprehensible charts. It might have been ordinary, or even child's play to a mathematician, but it was nonsense to Anna, who was looking for letters, diaries, or phone numbers. Even a dog-eared Valentine would have done. It was like looking for a pin-up in a stamp collection.

She gave up and went downstairs.

Mrs Hahn, now dressed in a cream silk suit, was perched on the edge of a leather chesterfield giving Mrs Elder instructions about lunch.

'Well?' Mrs Hahn said as the older woman left, closing the door quietly behind her. 'Did you find anything helpful?'

Anna had the impression she knew to the last detail what Thea kept in her room, so she held out the list and said, 'Could I have the name of Thea's last school and any friends she stayed in touch with.'

'The school, by all means,' Mrs Hahn said, and added another name and address to the paper. 'But as to friends—well, you must understand that Thea did not mix with girls her own age. She was always several years ahead scholastically.'

'But didn't she have any hobbies?' Anna cast around for something that might do. 'Riding, music, dancing?'

Mrs Hahn smiled and said, 'I was fond of horses and dancing at her age. But Thea is afraid of horses. And of course young people don't dance these days. Well, not the sort Thea could be taught. She plays the piano quite well, I'm told. Oh, and of course chess.'

'Of course, chess,' Anna said. 'Who did she play with?'

'Her father's quite good, I believe. But even he wasn't much competition for her. No, we have a chess program for the computer. Would you like to see it? It's in the study.'

'No, thank you.' Anna sighed. Perhaps the chess program was an important clue. But if it was, she wouldn't understand it.

Kinsey Millhone is...

"The best new private eye." —*The Detroit News*

"A tough-cookie with a soft center." —*Newsweek*

"A stand-out specimen of the new female operatives."
—*Philadelphia Inquirer*

Sue Grafton is...

The Shamus and Anthony Award winning creator of Kinsey Millhone and quite simply one of the hottest new mystery writers around.

Bantam is...

The proud publisher of Sue Grafton's Kinsey Millhone mysteries: